MEET THE FORCE RECON TEAM . . .

JACK SWAYNE

The leader of the team. A brilliant tactician and superb soldier. For him, failure is not an option . . . ever.

GREINER

The Boy Scout. In the infantry battalion he won Marine of the Month—every month. And he's all too ready to test his mettle in the field.

NIGHT RUNNER

A full-blooded American Indian. Even with the cutting-edge technology used by the team, the deadliest thing about him is his senses.

FRIEL

An ex–street thug turned disciplined Marine. A natural-born killer with no remorse. Possibly the deadliest shot in the world.

FORCE RECON

The explosive military action series by
James V. Smith, Jr.

FORCE RECON

STALKING TIGER

James V. Smith, Jr.

BERKLEY BOOKS, NEW YORK

FORCE RECON: STALKING TIGER

A Berkley Book / published by arrangement with
the author

PRINTING HISTORY
Berkley edition / November 2003

Copyright © 2003 by James V. Smith, Jr.
Cover design by Steven Ferlauto.

ISBN: 0-425-19301-2

BERKLEY®
Berkley Books are published by The Berkley Publishing Group,
a division of Penguin Group (USA) Inc.,
375 Hudson Street, New York, New York 10014.
BERKLEY and the "B" design
are trademarks belonging to Penguin Group (USA) Inc.

PRINTED IN THE UNITED STATES OF AMERICA

10 9 8 7 6 5 4 3 2 1

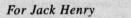

For Jack Henry

EVENT SCENARIO 22

"CHARLIE."

Captain Jack Swayne muttered the word into his radio mike, code telling the rest of his Force Recon team that he had spotted an enemy force that posed no threat to the Spartans.

In their simple code, a B word meant likely enemy contact, but with little danger. An A word warned of immediate danger from a serious threat.

Right now, the only threat was to the man he had spotted in his night vision binoculars, a young man and a good soldier, besides. For an enemy. The jungle had grown black as blindness itself since moonset an hour ago. Yet the kid performed his guard duty without slacking. He had not tried to loaf in the dark just because his noncom could not see him. He held his AK-47 Chinese model Kalashnikov rifle at port arms with his left hand as he walked around his mobile post. He kept touch with his duty by brushing his fingertips against

the camouflage paint of the truck and trailer as he walked.
A good kid. Too bad he had to die.

Swayne wiped at his dripping nose, thinking maybe the
kid just kept moving because of the damned cold. Swayne,
lying prone, his head bent over his NVGs, tried not to sniff
at the constant drizzle, knowing that the sound could be an-
noying over his open, sound-activated radio mike. He had
spent time on missions in Montana, Iraq, Iran, Kosovo, and
Afghanistan. Odd that the jungle, steamy by day, could be
so bone-wracking chilly at night. The hot day itself was
partly to blame, of course. His clothes had never dried out,
and the dampness wicked the heat away now.

He ordered his brittle, stilted fingers to record his settings,
confirming them one at a time in the heads-up view of the
binoculars. *Range, 206 meters. Azimuth, 044 degrees true.
Video to standby. Transmitter, engaged.*

Besides the standard laser range finder and designator that
could paint targets for smart bombs and other weapons sys-
tems, this latest version of NVG binoculars transmitted video
and used a remote GPS system in its dense electronics pack.
That meant a lot to this operation. It also recorded audio.

Which was a big deal to the rear echelon commandos in
the Operational Mission Command Center two hundred feet
below the surface of the ground at Quantico, Virginia. They
could watch like the war voyeur wanna-bes they were, so he
did not have to make a verbal report.

It also meant that two members of his team, Greiner and
Friel, could set up to provide all-round security. Positioned
ten meters to Swayne's left and right, they could watch the
flanks and rear in their own night vision goggles. But the
satellite also transmitted Swayne's image to his men. Their
goggles had a picture-in-picture view of the image transmitted by Swayne's NVGs. The PiP was a small screen that
could be made larger. They could also swap PiP images with
the actual view in their own goggles, the same as couch

potatoes watching two football games between beer com-
mercials all over America.

It also meant that Night Runner could watch pictures of
the young soldier as he closed in to kill him.

FOR ONCE NIGHT Runner didn't mind the gadgets. Usually
he relied on his senses to get around. That worked fine in
the deserts and temperate forests where he had operated on
his missions of the last few years. He felt as out of place in
the tropics as a grizzly—or a Blackfeet warrior—in the city.
Except for some training exercises, the Spartans hadn't
worked the jungles much. So he welcomed the lightweight
NVGs that opened up the dense world beneath the triple-
canopy jungle. He liked the idea of the PiP view in his goggles, which gave him the ability to watch a target from a
distance. Whether that truck was fifty meters or fifty miles
away did not matter. Because Swayne's NVGs were looking
at it, so was he.

Even more than the technology, he liked his companion,
Monty.

Since only yesterday, he'd come to admire the slight figure
now darting ahead of him through the foliage, as much a
shadow as a man.

For the first time, Gunnery Sergeant Robert Night Runner
began to understand why the men in Force Recon team 2400
thought of him, Runner, as a supernatural Marine. He felt
the same way about the dark-skinned aboriginal man who
flitted in total darkness without the aid of night vision goggles. Not counting the Kalashnikov slung over his shoulder
and a bandoleer of ammo clips and rations strapped across
his chest, he wore nothing but a pair of gray briefs. The
underwear fit tightly down the thighs about four inches. Old
Navy, of all things, was stitched across one lean cheek of
the briefs. He darted along in silence, weaving among
branches and twigs like a modern dancer on a stage without
scenery. He did not even stir the air in his wake, for not even

the most flimsy of leaves trembled as he passed by.

And so quietly. Like a shadow. Or, as Friel would say, a silent fart.

Night Runner realized the secret had to be in walking bare-foot. He had taken that concept as far as he could already. He had asked the tekkies to develop boots for him two years ago. The extra-soft soles and thin leather uppers wrapped like a second skin around his sockless feet gave him a good feel for the ground. Friel mocked them as spray-painted boots. But, quiet as they were, and as sensitive as they allowed his feet to be, Night Runner had never been able to creep through the forest like this aboriginal man of Asia.

At times the Montagnard put his feet down like a stalking water bird, sliding the toe forward beneath the live foliage, dried leaves, and dead twigs, wearing the ground cover like a stocking. Somehow, he lifted his foot backward, sliding his foot out so the forest debris fell back into place without leaving a print. Other times, he walked across a bed of dry, broken sticks without breaking one. Tough as the skin on his feet was, he seemed to be able to sense every twig that might snap. Without even halting, he somehow shifted his weight from one side of his foot to the other or from heel to toe leaving the twigs for Night Runner to break.

Not that Night Runner was so noisy. He knew how to drift through a forest like a mist. He knew how to shift his weight without breaking stride. At his noisiest—when Monty led him across a stand of bamboo poles that had been cut down and left to lie on the ground like a dropped bag of giant spaghetti—Night Runner made no more noise than the jungle itself, which rattled, clattered, and clanked like a rhythm band.

Flying beetles big as mice caromed off the trees like golf tee shots into the forest. Overhead, birds and monkeys splashed through the leafy canopy, sometimes hooting, squawking, or yapping, sometimes all three. Branches, nuts, and fruits pelted the ground, crashing in the litter on the forest floor. So Runner was not abashed at the noise he made. Instead, he was taken by the pure genius noiselessness of Monty, who moved without effort, without any special attempt to focus, like a city dweller strolling down the sidewalk to buy a Sunday paper at the corner stand. As inconspicuous and down home as a Montana rancher on the way to the barn.

Until tonight, Night Runner had never watched anybody perform better than himself in matters of stealth. One man, a Bedouin, had come close several missions ago. Runner had been forced to draw upon every ounce of skill and wit to defeat the terrorist scout inside Iraq. He was glad this Monty was not his enemy. Because as good as Night Runner was, he realized the aboriginal man had him beat. Night Runner might be a Blackfeet warrior with a heritage of stealth leading back to men who fought the frontier army of General Custer and beyond. But he was only a man. Monty was a bird of prey, virtually a spirit with the eyes and wings of an owl, able to turn day into night, able to glide over a carpet of cellophane without a sound. Yes, the men of his Force Recon team thought Night Runner was something special. Wait until they saw this guy in action.

Runner checked the PiP view in the left corner of his night vision goggles. The enemy sentry had moved into frame, still keeping touch with the skin of his vehicle. Already the truck had halted five minutes for refueling. If the tiny convoy held to the form that Monty had reported, it would be on the move again in ten to twenty minutes. The sentry's night vision had not yet adjusted. Night Runner read the numbers in the heads-up display. They told him that Monty was on course— of course—now closing to within twenty meters of the truck.

Monty stopped, one leg frozen above the foliage ahead of him. By instinct, Night Runner made a quick halt-and-glance sweeping survey to the right flank, the rear, to the left flank. Then he looked back at his guide. Had he heard something? No.

He finally saw the snake in front of Monty, flattened sides, broad head, with scales heavy and regular as chain mail. A bamboo viper, the pale green color of its namesake plant, lying like a swerving, curvy road on a map. Night Runner's color-capable goggles could barely make out the image against the forest floor. *How could Monty do that in the dark?*

Without calling attention to it, the man turned, stepped left, and continued on his silent way, leaving Night Runner amazed once again. The back he had been watching was broad and muscular. But when Monty turned sideways, he nearly disappeared because he was such a thin man from chest to spine.

Ten meters later, he stopped and looked over his shoulder, smiling at Night Runner. Like his back, Monty's head was broad. He had a pie-pan face, a flattened, flared nose, and a gaping, toothy smile big as a tiger's. His eyes seemed set too far apart. Then again, maybe that was what gave him his spectacular binocular vision at night. Maybe he truly was the unfeathered owl of the Asian forest. Monty beckoned, his palm toward the ground, fingers pointed downward, fanning the earth in the way of Vietnamese people. He pointed from his piano keyboard smile to his teacup ears.

Runner closed up.

"Just ahead of us," said Monty in French. "About ten meters. Two men, one sitting, one walking. One tanker. One truck. One trailer. One missile." He punctuated his report by jabbing the proper number of fingers at Night Runner.

Two men? Night Runner had not seen a second man on his PiP screen. The captain had not said anything about anybody remaining behind with the sentry. The overhead satellite told them nothing; it could not see through the jungle canopy, in either visual or thermal mode.

Night Runner checked the GPS readout in his NVGs, accurate to within half a meter. It read: *9.6 m.*, about thirty feet. Swayne's night vision binoculars had calculated the azimuth and distance from its position to the truck, arriving at a precise coordinate for the target. It had sent the data to a satellite, which relayed the information to Runner's own NVGs. The GPS in his instrument package calculated his position and gave him an azimuth, distance, and real-time picture of the target. In the digital age, things did not get lost in the translation of coordinates. Yet he trusted Monty more than the machines.

He translated from French to English and told the captain what Monty had reported.

"How does he know there's a second man?" Swayne asked.

A fair question. Night Runner relayed it in French.

Monty smiled big and moved in close enough to press against Night Runner. Runner held his ground. He understood that most Asians did not have the same sense of personal space as Westerners, so he did not cringe, although the pungent scent of fish sauce and garlic forced him to hold his breath.

"I smelt one stink-ass Vietcong." Monty spoke in English, as if to make his point stronger by using Night Runner's language. "Den I smelt one stink-ass snake, and den I smelt two stink-ass Vietcong," he said, answering both of Night Runner's questions at once.

"ROGER," SAID SWAYNE before the Gunny could draw breath to answer. He had heard the report through Night Runner's microphone. He cranked the new data into his well-laid plan, little more than a cold hope now that a worm had infected it.

He had a choice: scrap the mission now, or factor in the second man, deal with him, and blow the missile in place. This should have been a short mission. Left to his team, they'd be done with it, already on the way to their pickup point. But, no, the desk commandos wanted them to make it look like an accident.

He murmured into his microphone, "Spartan Three, Spartan Four, any sign of the second guy?"

"Spartan Three, negative."

"Spartan Four, negative."

Swayne shook his head in dismay. He should have been glad that his men gave him succinct answers. He wasn't. First, he wanted to know why none of them had seen a second man. Without the Montagnard guide, Night Runner would have gone in to sabotage the missile, according to their plan. Then, if the second man put in his appearance, very likely, the operation would have blown up in their faces. At no little risk to the gunny.

His second concern was Spartan Three. Sergeant Henry Friel had answered in only one word. Usually he had nothing less than a mouthful to say. *What the hell is his problem now?*

Third, was there really an extra soldier down there? Was the Montagnard reliable? Or was he merely so clever an enemy agent that he would invent a second soldier just to make the Americans back off? It could be more effective than betraying them with noise or even turning his rifle on them.

Swayne, deep in thought about those questions, suddenly realized that somebody had asked him another one.

"This is Spartan One, say again."

"Request instructions?" Night Runner, speaking in a hushed voice, had spoken volumes. *Get off the dime. Do something. Tell me what to do. Stay or go?*

"Stand by." Swayne needed a moment. At least that's what he told himself. He needed to know whether anything had changed with the rest of the small convoy. One security vehicle, a three-quarter-ton truck with ten men, had preceded the tractor trailer. It had stopped two hundred meters up the road. A second truckload of soldiers followed the main convoy at the same distance exactly as the Montagnard had told them it would happen. This was a rest and refueling stop. After spending the daylight under cover of canopy, the convoy of the tractor trailer and its precious cargo would be escorted by security forces down the old Ho Chi Minh Trail of the new Vietnam. He had said it would arrive at this rest station about eight hours later, change crews, refuel vehicles, allow the men to prepare their own meals alongside the road, and continue the journey after a thirty- to forty-five-minute stop. So far, everything had gone according to the Montagnard's timetable. Of course, that did not prove he was one of the good guys. In fact, he was too on-point with his intel, giving Swayne doubts he could not suppress. Only the Vietnamese themselves would be more exact.

If it were not for the video record he was shooting, Swayne might have taken another tack. Tell Night Runner to place explosive charges on the truck and the missile, give him time to clear the area, and set them off by remote. Who was to say that there had not been a spark near a leak of the rocket propellant? Accident enough for Swayne. But the damned video. It was more than silent commo. It was a digital picture record playing to an audience in the OMCC. Copies might end up in the hands of select members of Congress and the administration staff. The CIA would know and disapprove of something as direct as planting charges and calling it an accident. Real spooks used complex tricks and shady deals. Why walk up to the front door and knock when you could rappel a fireproof agent down the chimney right into a bucket of roasting chestnuts?

But Swayne had no tricks to play. For that matter, although he lay just two hundred meters away from the action, he lacked the nitty-gritty even to butt in. Runner stood just a few feet away from the target, smelling the dragon's breath. This was not Swayne's decision to make.

"Spartan Two, this is One. Your call."

NIGHT RUNNER STOOD with his body against a tree, becoming one with its trunk. In turn, the Montagnard leaned against him, pressing his head against Night Runner's, picking up

10   JAMES V. SMITH, JR.

whatever sound that leaked from the receiver plugged into
Night Runner's ear.

Although he understood it, Night Runner was annoyed by
the closeness. Not so much at the invasion of his personal
space, which did bother him some. But more because he
could not pick up the scent of that second man. Too much
smell of garlic and fish exuded from Monty.

At Swayne's transmission, Monty pulled away, smiling
and nodding. "You betcha," said the thin man in his rough
English. "More better you do it. I help."

Night Runner murmured into the man's satellite dish ear.
"If I take the sentry, can you take the second man?"

Monty's answer was the magician's flourish of one hand.
He produced a switchblade knife from one of the magazine
pouches of his bandoleer. A touch of the button and flash of
the blade made Night Runner flinch. The Montagnard caught
the blade with one finger and eased it fully open so it could
not make its trademark metallic snap as it locked into place.
As he held the flat of the blade against his flared nostrils,
Monty's eyes glittered on either side of the stiletto point.

Night Runner liked Monty, but he had been in too many
scrapes to trust a man he had known for only a couple of
days. He clasped both his hands over the broad, dark hand
of the Montagnard. He had calluses on the knotty knuckles
as well as the palms.

"No noise," he said in French. "Can you do this without
making a lot of noise?"

Monty closed the knife. "You betcha." His smile melded
into a wicked glimmer of teeth. "No damn stink-ass VC
noise."

Suddenly the man's eyes narrowed. He put the knife handle to his lips to signal for silence. Night Runner heard the
crew returning to the tractor to refuel it, just as the Montagnard said they would. There was still time enough to carry
off the attack. But not much.

"Where is the second VC?" Night Runner asked.

In a single motion, the Montagnard shrugged and tapped the side of his nose with one finger. In French, he said, "I cannot see him. I can only smell him, at the front someplace. Take care of the sentry and the truck. I will do the rest. Depend on it."

Night Runner watched as Monty crept toward the cab of the truck, his nose held high to stay on the scent of his man. Amazing. He felt a twinge of envy. Imagine. Navigating by his nose.

He spoke into his microphone, "Spartan Three, keep an eye on the refueling party for me."

"WILCO," SAID SERGEANT Henry Friel. At Swayne's left flank, Friel could see the picnic area under the canopy where the Vietnamese gathered to smoke and joke—just like any other military mooks he had known. Same stuff in the Marines, the Navy, the Army, and the Air Force, which was almost one of the armed services. You put a bunch of guys in uniform, and they all acted the same way. Call a break time and watch them slack off. Tell their little jokes. Suck down their little smokes. The gooks down there making funny about their officers, bragging about how many times they puked the last time they got drunk, and lying about getting laid. Same deal with the grunts in the armies of Iran, Iraq, Kosovo, and al Qaida in Afghanistan. If all these mooks met each other and realized how much they had in common, would they keep on fighting each other? Probably. People could always find crap to fight and kill about. *Die, you blue-eyed bastard, said the boys in the brown-eyed band.*

Friel had to admit it. He didn't think the same about things anymore. He had changed enough since his first time out with the Force Recon team that his own mother would turn him in—*Where's my Henry, you alien bastard fake.* He had watched his first gunnery sergeant die while saving Friel's life from enemy fire. His next gunnery sergeant—that was Night Runner—had thrown him naked into the line of fire.

The Marines had court-martialed the gunny and almost kicked Friel out of the Corps as a head case after that one.

Last mission, he had nearly done himself in. Landing wrong after a parachute jump under fire. Breaking his own jaw when his knees buckled. Slamming into his weapon, jamming it into his kisser. The whole mission inside Afghanistan a freaking dream. Night Runner had set his jaw by wrapping bad-ass duct tape around his face. Then, after Friel had gotten two six-pack sick, the Gunny had to cut through the tape—and his lips—widening his mouth so he would not drown in his own puke.

Once back in the land of the free, dental surgeons had wired his teeth shut, and plastic surgeons had repaired his face. With months of enforced silence until the wires were removed, Friel had, for the first time in his life, done more thinking than talking. He had decided, now that he could talk, he would listen more than he used to, mess with a few minds. His attitude hadn't changed any. Just that he did not have to say as much; the surgery on his face had left a wise-ass smirk that said it all. It was almost worth it. The new look pissed off every officer he saluted. Officers. They couldn't stand it when you gave them smart-ass looks, even when you couldn't help it.

Or so he told himself.

One thing for sure. He could pull an officer's chain now by just looking at him. Or saying one innocent word. That was more fun than needling the brass with buckets of smart-ass. He knew what was going on in Swayne's head. The new Friel had answered *"Wilco."* The shortest possible way of saying, *I understand my orders and will comply.* The new Friel's smirk wrinkled even more than usual in the dark. The new Friel loved screwing with the mind of the old captain.

The old Friel would have bugged the hell out of the man. He would have been asking to go weapons-hot to put a 20 mm round into the missile. Or the picnic area. The old Friel would have been pushing Swayne, ragging on his ass for

wasting time trying to noodle things out. That was the captain, always trying to figure the angles. The old Friel figured
it was better to pop a cap, start a fight, make a move—
anything but sit on your ass and wait for things to happen
on their own. Better to *make* things happen. Initiate. Insti-
gate. Stimulate. Then go with the flow. Break some glass.
Play some games. Kick some ass. Take some names: Oh,
yeah, baby. But that was the old Friel.

Or so he told himself. Just as he spotted a new wrinkle.

Three of the Vietnamese in the picnic area stubbed out
their butts. Smoke-break over. Now. If that little pizza-face
anorexic screwball Eskimo in the Speedo was right about it,
they were the refueling team. In about two minutes, they
were going to be at the truck. Which was where the chief
was supposed to be. The old Friel would have given an entire
lecture. Just to screw with the captain's head, he gave his
report in code: "Banzai, three bandits at your six."

NIGHT RUNNER SMILED. He knew well enough that Friel
hadn't forgotten how to bullshit over the radio. All those
months with his face wired shut, he had learned to smart off
with facial expressions and body language. Someday he was
going to be as mouthy as ever. Until then, might as well
enjoy the man's radio discipline, faked or otherwise.

Night Runner had learned a lot from Friel's six-word report. An enemy force of three was approaching his position
from the rear of the trailer as he lay between six sets of dual
tires of the rig. Beside him lay the Montagnard. So far, the
thin man had been correct about everything. He had also
found the second man, the one not accounted for by the video
camera, asleep in the cab of the truck. The thin man had
followed his nose out of the jungle and across the new Ho
Chi Minh Trail. He had stepped up onto the running board
of the truck and peeked inside, turning to smile wide as Julia
Roberts, looking for all the world as if he had too many teeth,

a whole packet of unchewed Chiclets plastered across the front of his mouth.

Night Runner waved for Monty to join him beneath the truck. The sentry was on the far side but would soon be coming around. Whereas the guard worked in the dark, the refueling crew showed much less discipline. Two flashlights with red lens covers splattered the overhanging foliage like a lame laser light show at a rock concert. Night Runner worried that a stray beam might catch them.

His heart stopped when the sentry called out.

A gnarly hand touched his forearm. "He told them two shit VC to cover their flashlights," said Monty, translating the Vietnamese into French.

Night Runner dared to breathe. But he did not feel all that much relief. Somehow, they had to deal with the sentry, three support troops, and a man in the cab of the truck. Destroy the equipment, kill the men. And, oh, by the way, make it all look like an accident besides. He wished he could set loose the Beltway boneheads in this situation. Stand back and watch. See how they handle it, see if they could rescue an accident out of an imminent disaster.

SWAYNE WATCHED THE situation unfold through his NVGs. The three men walked to the far side of the truck, out of sight. He knew what was there. A rubberized fabric bladder, four meters by twelve meters, lay on a slightly larger, squared-off mound of earth. The mound elevated the fuel bladder to about five feet above ground level. He knew from studying the history of the Vietnam War that such bladders had been dug into the ground and sandbagged around the edges. Each might hold more than ten thousand gallons of aircraft fuel during the war. Trucks or helicopters would bring in smaller bladders of fuel, two hundred fifty or five hundred, whatever they could carry. The smaller soft containers would be drained into the large bladder and carried back for refilling. American forces would throw up sandbags around the edges of the huge bladders, run hoses, set up pumps, string concertina wire, lay on some security, and have a major helicopter refueling site in operation in an afternoon. Here under the canopy, with no war and no threat of ground attack, the bladder could be elevated. The Ho Chi Minh Trail probably had such gravity-fed gas stations every hundred miles. He did not doubt that they were even more plentiful than service stations along Vietnam's open roads.

In a few minutes, there would be one less Vietnamese Esso station in service. Night Runner would see to it.

NIGHT RUNNER KEPT up with the situation to make sure things came off the way Monty briefed them. One of the fuel handlers would run the main valve at the bladder, according to Monty. The second man would refuel the saddle tank on the driver's side first. The third man would stand off and smoke, waiting for his turn to go to work. When the driver's saddle tank was full, the first refueler would take his cigarette break. The third man would take over. He'd drag the hose forward of the truck and around to the saddle tank on the passenger side. The sentry would continue to walk. With luck, the man in the cab would continue to sleep.

Night Runner peeked out from the space between the dual driving tires. He needed everybody to be in the proper position for his "accident" to come off as planned. The sentry should be at the rear or the front of the truck. The man on smoke break would have to stand far enough away or have his head turned for just a moment.

But the Vietnamese were not playing along. The man at the fuel bladder turned the valve to allow the main flow, then joined his companion on smoke break. The sentry stopped to chat with the man refueling on the driver's side. When he moved on after a minute or so, a new voice spoke up from inside the cab; the sleeping man had been roused. So much for Plan A.

Night Runner fought back a stirring of impatience. He

glanced at his watch. Ten minutes more, twenty, tops. The truck would roll on, if he didn't pull this off, literally leaving him in the dust. He bit his lip. Still time. Plenty of time. No need to panic. The Montagnard tapped at his elbow. Night Runner lent his ear. Monty whispered in French. Night Runner nodded. It was a better idea than any he had, and worth a try. Anything was better than lying here waiting for the enemy to get with his program. He watched the Montagnard slither away on his belly. Amazing. Quiet as that viper.

SWAYNE WATCHED WHAT little he could see, as the action unfolded. A movement behind the three sets of driving wheels revealed finally where Night Runner was. No, the Montagnard slipped out from behind the tires and stood up, his back to the trailer chassis. Swayne touched the toggle switch on his NVGs and zoomed in to confirm what he thought he saw. Yes, the thin man stood there grinning, his teeth like beacons, as the sentry came around the front of the truck, trailing his fingers on the metal. The Montagnard did not move as the sentry approached. Didn't the Montagnard see what was going on? If he was trying to stay out of sight, he was going to be discovered by a touch of the hand. Maybe the bastard was a spy, after all, an enemy agent about to give a signal to the soldier.

Swayne opened his mouth to tell Friel to put a bead on the son of a bitch.

He clapped his lips shut on the order. Now was not the time to butt into a situation and give Night Runner something else to worry about. He raised his own rifle and laid the night scope on the bare, shiny chest of the Montagnard. He couldn't shoot like Friel, but hell, this was only two hundred meters.

A moment later he was glad that he kept his mouth shut and did not disturb Night Runner. The Montagnard grinned wider as the sentry approached. Clearly, he saw the Vietnamese soldier and knew that he would not be seen. He let the soldier pass by, let the fingers run across his chest. He watched the soldier recoil from the touch of human skin. As the Vietnamese sentry leaped away and tried to bring his Kalashnikov to bear, the Montagnard stepped into him. With his right hand, he grasped the trigger guard, so the soldier's right hand had no place to grip. A short jab to the throat with the off hand, fist swift as a python's strike, dropped the sentry to the ground, leaving his rifle in the hands of the fighter known as Monty.

Swayne marveled at the power and speed of the attack. He listened for Friel to make some remark on it, but not a word from the smart-ass department.

NIGHT RUNNER WAITED until he saw spindly legs and broad, flat feet step up onto the running board on the passenger side. Like Swayne, he was impressed with the speed of the attack, which he had seen only as action from the hips down. He had no time to dwell on emotion. They had taken the first, fatal step. From now on only actions mattered. The operation would look like an accident only if the team took out all witnesses and evidence. So he set to his task.

He carried only his 9 mm pistol, two boomer grenades, a bayonet, and a length of piano wire. Also, his terrible swift sword, which he had taken off the Bedouin in Iraq. For his part in Monty's plan, he would use the bayonet.

The action was over inside a minute. It began when the man inside the cab gave a little yelp.

The refueler looked up toward the side window at the driver's seat. As he exposed his throat, Night Runner stood up, bringing up his bayonet. Into the soft spot beneath the chin, through the tongue, driving it up through the soft palate and into the brain. The man did not even fall; Night Runner supported him with the hilt of his bayonet. He took the refueling nozzle away with the other hand. He laid the nozzle, still shooting a stream of diesel on the ground beneath the cab. Monty called out from the cab in Vietnamese, which

Night Runner did not understand, and French, which he did.

"I have a wallet full of money," Monty hollered. "Hundreds. Does it belong to one of you?"

The news brought the pair running, calling out as if they'd both lost the same wallet. Night Runner switched hands, holding up his man with his left hand so he could withdraw his bayonet with the right. He stood behind the dead man, waiting to strike again.

SWAYNE SQUIRMED. HE didn't like the idea that, even with all the high-dollar toys, he was blind. Dammit, what was happening on the dark side of that truck?

He could not count the number of times that he had seen mishaps gang up on a mission all at once. At some nickel-and-dime point in every operation—and he had not found a way to identify such a moment in advance—things just went to shit. With this one, the extra Vietnamese soldier, whom he now knew was dead inside the cab of the truck, had seemed like a small enough problem. All at once a number of ducks began to nibble the operation to death. It began with the radio calls.

First Greiner: "Ambulance," he said, giving the A code for imminent enemy contact. "The advance party truck is flipping a U-y on the road—it's booking back toward the missile carrier."

Then Friel: "Assholes," he hissed, applying his Friel-ness to the code. "Rear guard is hauling ass, too."

Swayne slammed a fist into the ground. The satellite was supposed to be listening in on radio traffic from this spot. By now it should have—

Then the Operational Mission Control Center: "Spartan One this is Eagle. Sig analysts here say the security force commander just gave orders for everybody in the two escort detachments to converge on the refueling station."

Swayne gritted his teeth. About time. Where was that report a minute ago? What was going on behind that truck? If that wiry little Montagnard bastard had somehow jumped Night Runner and sounded an alarm—

The sentry laid out by Monty sat up, gagging for breath and holding his throat, inserting himself into the tangle.

"Want me to cap the rear guard?" Friel. At last, the Friel of old. Butting in at the worst possible moment.

"Negative." Swayne needed to hear from Night Runner before bailing on the plan to pull off a phony accident. "Spartan Two? SitRep?"

"STAND BY," SAID Night Runner. No time for a situation report. He had his hands full with the Vietnamese. Literally. First the dead man he held up.

Second the pair racing at him to claim the wallet full of cash. Monty opened the driver's door to the truck. One of the refuelers stopped short. He called out in Vietnamese, the tone high-pitched, afraid.

"Who am I?" Monty said in French. "I am your angel of death."

At that, the second man came to a halt. The nearest of the two was still beyond Runner's reach, even with the bayonet. So he dropped the dead weight of his shield and lunged at the two in the sharp-angled thrust of a fencer.

Before he could reach them with the tip of his blade, a lanky, nearly naked bird of prey flew past his shoulder, leaping from the cab of the truck, hitting the two Vietnamese, bowling both of them over.

Night Runner knelt beside then nearest one, putting the bayonet to his throat.

"Not necessary, my friend," Monty said in his fluent French. He finished in his broken English. "Dem two shit Vietcong sleep long time."

Night Runner pointed at one refueler. "Carry him over to the main fuel valve," he said in French. The captain did not speak French, but he would know that both Night Runner and the Montagnard were all right. He'd spoken so calmly.

What's more, his boom mike had picked up Monty's outburst in broken English about the sleeping enemy. More than enough of a SitRep for Swayne. Besides, Runner could hear trucks roaring toward them from both north and south. To use Friel's words, the fecal matter was about to hit the splatter fan.

Monty draped his man over one shoulder, his smile on high-beam though the man was nearly twice his size. Night Runner moved the bodies of the other two, staging the scene. He unclipped the copper grounding cable from the chassis of the truck and wrapped it around the leg of one man. The other he arranged into a sprawled position on his back. *A terrible accident, comrade, terrible.*

He picked up the fuel nozzle and sprayed diesel onto the truck and trailer, splashing the truck's tires. He tried not to spray it on the men.

A wasted gesture. They were going to die anyhow when the diesel went up. That he could not bring himself to wet them down gave him little comfort. Murder by another name, but murder just the same.

He ran to the fuel bladder, pulling a boomer grenade from his shirt pocket, preset to remote detonation. He armed it and placed it beneath the bladder. Monty had draped his payload over the shut-off valve to the refueling hose. A nice touch. It would look as if the man had been a hero, trying to stop the fuel flow. Runner shook his head in disgust with himself. A nice touch, indeed. What had happened to him? His last two bloody missions into Afghanistan, once with his team, one with Delta Force. Was he really a warrior? Or just a serial killer? No, worse yet, he'd become a terrorist, one of America's own.

As he turned, Night Runner saw headlights slashing through the trees. They had only seconds to clear the area. He caught a glimpse of Monty running around to the other side of the vehicle. He heard a fragment of English: ". . . shit VC."

The sound of engines revving to the red line told Night Runner he'd run out of time. These people weren't coming back for tea and rice cakes. This was the cavalry. Somebody had set off an alarm.

The plan was to touch a match to a trickle of fuel. But he could smell a dense, invisible cloud of fuel fog. He dared not risk a spark now. The whole sham of an accidental fire was lost if the body of a Force Recon Marine gunnery sergeant turned up among the dead. Some accident. Whose damned stupid idea was that anyhow? He armed his second boomer and dropped it into the open fuel tank. Then, juiced by adrenaline, he sprinted across the road, diving into the foliage as one set of headlights from his left, then another from the right, swept the road.

Branches whipped his face. They'd seen him, surely. He landed on his chest, hard. Something, a stone or a branch, drove into his sternum, knocking him breathless. For a second, he felt gut-shot. He rolled away and patted down his belly. No blood. He felt the smooth stone that had struck him. The stone grew legs and lumbered away. He gasped but could draw no air. Then again. He didn't need. Air. He needed to get clear. If they saw him. They'd shoot up the . . . forest. Where. He. Went. In.

He crawled away as fast as he could. Lumbering like the turtle. Until his vision grew dim. He lay down and groaned, "Mon . . . ty?"

"He's in the clear." Swayne's voice was tiny in Runner's ear-receiver. "He carried the sentry and his rifle away from the truck." Then, in a voice from the end of the earth, "Gunny? You okay?"

Night Runner grunted. He pulled out his remote detonator, no larger than the remote on his Land Rover key chain back home. He thumbed a switch to the Fire position. Darkness closed in on him as he rolled onto his side.

Through a tunnel of vision and foliage, Night Runner saw both vehicles race up to the tractor trailer and its payload, keeping to the road. So far they hadn't seen their own men lying on the other side of the truck.

He reviewed the triangle of three buttons. How did that go again? The top button the Arm button? The left button set to the grenade that had come from the left pocket of his jacket, the one beneath the bladder? The grenade from his right pocket, he had placed into the fuel tank?

As the men disgorged from their two trucks, the tunnel shrank around his vision. He put his left thumb to the Arm button and held it down. Some accident. The Vietnamese were supposed to get the idea that a spark had set off an explosion. If a man tripped over the wire—what a joke. Anybody who watched the CSI shows—

Runner's lips went numb.

He thought he heard Swayne call to him. He mashed the right button while he still could.

SWAYNE SAW IT all—without the night vision goggles, because the flash would wash out the image. The orange yellow burst rolled into the sky as a fireball that soon vanished into its own black mushroom cloud that melded into the dark of the sky. From the moment the fire engulfed the truck, he could see that the main part of the mission had been accomplished. That truck, that trailer, that missile would never be recovered.

Men on the ground ran away, fearful that the missile might explode. Swayne knew better. The cargo rode too high on its springs for it to be full of propellant. Besides, nobody would be stupid enough to carry such a volatile cargo along such a primitive road as the new Ho Chi Minh Trail. Even if the missile did not develop a leak and endanger everybody, the sheer weight of it would wreck the road after the delivery of no more than three missiles to the southern provinces, where apparently this one was headed. Likewise, the missiles were not armed with explosive warheads. A blunt cylinder covered the opening where a pointed nose would go. The warheads could be transported on hardball highways in ordinary cargo trailers, out of sight of spy satellites. Only the missiles, such as the one now melting into the pool of flames below him, would have to be moved secretly. Even from this distance, he could feel a warmth radiating from the spot. It took the chill off the night, and he was grateful for it. He hoped that Night Runner had moved far enough away, in case the forest caught on fire. Then again, why hadn't he set off the second blast?

"Runner," he called, keeping his voice calm. No reply.

"Gunny," he shouted, and to hell with the breach of noise discipline. "Are you okay?"

NIGHT RUNNER AWOKE to a new set of problems. Swayne shouting. Men running away from the explosion, crashing into the forest nearby. Right now, one of them was less than five meters away, although the undergrowth near the road was so dense, the soldier would not detect him. Runner had found his breath but lost the Montagnard. He was also more than a little concerned that one man, an officer from his demeanor, had run toward the fire. At first he thought the man might be looking for evidence of sabotage. He positioned his fingers so he could set off the second explosion. That he did not want to do; he was too near the bladder himself and did not dare to broil Monty. When it went off, the exploding lake of fire would pour his way, crossing the road like a tidal wave, spilling into the ditch where he now crouched. With so many soldiers around, he did not want to be seen running. They all had weapons, and there was no telling about their state of discipline. They might shoot at anything that moved in the jungle, including each other.

The officer, holding up his elbow to shield his face against the fire's intense heat, was forcing the issue on Night Runner. Once the man's eyes adjusted, he would see the unconscious soldier that Monty had draped over the shut-off valve. Then he would know this was no accident. Night Runner had no

choice. He touched off the second grenade. He got to his feet
and turned to sprint away without knowing for sure that he
could even run. His chest hurt, but his legs worked. The
flames lit his way. He began to jog. Until he felt a sunburn
on his neck. Jogging wasn't enough. He'd have to run like
hell to get out of the inferno he had just created.

SWAYNE WATCHED THE bladder go up in a spectacular blast
of light and flame, a shower of fire. He felt the warmth of
an open blaze first, then a second later, the noise hit him, the
sound of a gas barbecue grill touched off ten seconds too
late, but magnified a thousand times.

"Shit's sake, Chief, you okay?" said Friel.

Swayne seconded the question. "Night Runner?" he asked.
If he could feel the heat all the way up here—

"Ten-by." Night Runner said, his breathing choppy.

"The Montagnard?" Swayne asked.

NIGHT RUNNER DID not answer.

He had dared to glance over his shoulder. He saw a flood
of flames rolling like a fiery tide beneath the truck, swirling
around it, spreading up and down the road, sending the Vietnamese screaming deeper into the jungle. At his feet he saw
something else. He bent over and picked it up before dashing
through the trees again.

To his right and left men crashed through the forest. They
no longer cared if an enemy lurked in the forest. They ran,
not from the possibility of an enemy but the certainty of
death in the flaming tidal wave behind them. They ran for
their lives, ran from the living hell splashing into the woods
after them. None of them ran faster than Night Runner.

He did not know where he was going exactly. He tried to
remember the terrain. Sooner or later there should be an incline, the slope that he and Monty had come down as they
stalked the refueling site. To his left, a man cried out and
fell. He lay screaming, crying for help in his own language.

Night Runner did not understand the Vietnamese, just the terror. He sprinted even faster, aware of birds, monkeys, and small mammals crashing through the forest overhead, beside him, and even under his feet. Everybody, enemy and foe alike, man and beast, bird and snake, wanted nothing more or less than to escape the wall of fire licking at their tails. Night Runner felt a surge of panic. It urged him to throw away his burden that he had picked off the forest floor and save himself, but he held on.

He heard the screams choked off behind him as one man inhaled the fire. The Marine sergeant kept humping, feeling his knees begin to buckle, knowing that he had finally found the slope, hoping it was not too late, fearing that he might fall. He was gaining high ground now. Fire licked at his heels. He wanted to slap at the flames on the backs off his legs. But his hands were full. And he would not free them. He kept going until he was sure that the fire could not follow him, washing up the slope like a beached tsunami.

He knew he had reached a safe elevation when the heat on his back began to chill. Finding a thicket, he set down his load and tore off his gear and stripped his smoking jacket, wrapping it around his smoldering pant legs. The irony of the pun caused him to smile. Literally a smoking jacket. He kept his composure well enough not to look back into the bright light of the fire, already burning over the damp forest. The fuel had found a stream and had begun to flow deep into the woods downslope, where it would gradually burn itself out. He could hear firecrackers in the distance, small arms ammunition cooking off in the heat, and one or two explosions of fuel tanks and maybe rocket-propelled grenades.

The politicians had their accident, an accident for the ages.

His next concern was to find his companion. Above him on the slope he heard a sound, a crushing of leaves. He did not think it could be the Montagnard. The man was too quiet for that.

He heard a voice calling out in Vietnamese. He drew his pistol. Then the voice spoke in French, and he holstered the 9 mm beneath his armpit.

"Where are you my friend?" The voice repeated in French, then spoke again in Vietnamese.

Night Runner recognized the voice. Monty somehow had escaped. By using both languages, he could speak to Night Runner without drawing fire from the Vietnamese.

Runner spoke in French. Monty dropped the sentry onto the forest floor at Runner's feet and gave a broad grin. The Montagnard had carried the sentry away from the scene of the fire, no doubt so his body would not give away the sabotage if he were seen lying beside the truck before it exploded. Night Runner smiled, both at the man's ability to keep his wits about him and marveling at his strength for being able to carry the dead man this deep into the forest with that fire nipping at his heels.

He could have left the sentry behind to be engulfed by the flames. No doubt several bodies now lay cremating in the forest. It would take a long time for one of them to the sorted from another. Besides, once the Vietnamese saw that shrapnel had blown from inside the fuel tank, there'd be no mystery.

The sentry groaned, coming back to consciousness, breathing raggedly through his damaged throat.

"Do we need him any longer?" Monty asked in French. The question was punctuated by the metallic snap of the switchblade opening. He looked around. "They won't find him until the tigers have devoured him, and the ants have polished the remains."

For a moment, Night Runner felt as if he were one of the Roman emperors at the Colosseum. In his hands was this man's life. A shake of his head, and he would be dead. He did not like the power. "Let's take him with us," he said. He didn't know why. He just knew that he did not want to murder the man outright. In a fight, yes. Not like this. He stepped over the land turtle that he'd carried up the hill to safety. Perhaps another pointless gesture, that, saving the turtle's life. But better than leaving it to die.

MOMENTS AFTER HEARING that Night Runner and the Montagnard were safe, Swayne switched his night vision binoculars to daytime mode. As long as the intelligence satellites were going to get overhead pictures of a fire hot as the sun, he might as well photograph it from a low angle, too, and transmit pictures. If he didn't, some desk Rambo would accuse him of trying to hide the debacle. The politicians had demanded an accident. He had given them a full blown calamity.

In a way, it was funny. If it weren't for the ass chewing that he was going to get from Zavello, the whole thing would be just shy of slapstick comical. This is what happened when wanna-be soldiers fought their wars during wet dreams between their Egyptian cotton sheets, joystick in one hand and a prescription bottle of Viagra in the other. Imagine Ike getting orders from a bunch of political weenies in 1944: *Hit the beaches at Normandy and kick Hitler's ass all over Europe—oh, and, if it's not too much trouble, make it look like an accident.*

One thing for sure: the Vietnamese were going to have to wait a long time before they could sift through the ashes of this mess and determine it was no accident. Whether they figured it out or not, it was ridiculous for people in the chain of command to put combat teams into situations where they had to combine violent combat action with plausible denial.

Just three weeks ago, the CIA reported a movement of medium-range ballistic missiles by sea from China to the port Haiphong in Vietnam. Nobody had actually seen the missiles, either on the ground or by using satellites. But analysts had spotted an unusually long tractor trailer combination being off-loaded at the port. They argued that it could only be used to transport missiles like the Scuds fired into Israel and

Saudi Arabia during the Gulf War. Political advisers in the administration countered that Vietnam would not dare deploy such weapons that might unsettle the region, surely. Trade with the former enemy looked promising. Veterans' groups and junkets by members of Congress had proven that, hadn't they?

Besides, America had its hands full in a full-fledged global antiterrorist effort. It would not be convenient to be accused of trying to police the world. Especially not in place like Vietnam. The very mention of the country's name stirred up radicals on the faculties of campuses from one end of America—and Canada—to the other. Nobody on either side of the aisle in Congress wanted to take the heat for *another* another Vietnam. The term had already been applied to Saudi Arabia, Somalia, Afghanistan, Iraq, Iran, Canada, and Mexico. What could be worse than another Vietnam in Vietnam? So nobody would allow themselves to see, hear, and especially speak any evil concerning the People's Republic.

Yet, Thailand, America's only ally in the region, reported more than one firsthand account of missiles moving, one at a time, down the secret road through the jungle. The Vietnamese had built a modern Ho Chi Minh Trail. Once, during the sixties and seventies, the main artery and dozens of branch roads had been Main Street Vietnam under the canopy. No matter how hard U.S. Air Forces had tried to interdict it, the traffic kept flowing, delivering PAVN armies and resupply. Now, the Thai Secret Service reported a strategic application: missiles being installed all along Vietnam's border with Laos and Cambodia, missiles capable of hitting Bangkok.

So Swayne's Force Recon Team 2400, called Team Midnight for the obvious reason, had been sent into the country to meet up with an agent hired by the Thais. The team's mission? To prove that neither the new Ho Chi Minh Trail nor the missiles existed.

Just an hour earlier, Swayne had failed in that part of his

mission with a verbal report to the OMCC: "I'm looking at the tractor, the trailer, and a Scud-9 missile. From the hydraulics setup on the trailer, it looks like a mobile launch pad."

Colonel Karl Zavello, his irascible boss, had demanded proof. "Spartan One, this is Eagle One," he growled. "I need pictures."

Swayne did not take offense. Zavello believed him. Those higher in the chain of command, especially those with political concerns, needed more than the word of a Marine captain. They needed twenty-four thousand words a second, in the form of moving digital images, if you please.

Half an hour later, Zavello was back at him, telling him to carry out contingency Alpha-One. The pols had let their hope get out of hand, sending him to Vietnam with only instructions to disprove a claim.

Beforehand, back at Quantico, Swayne and Zavello had asked themselves the question: What if the missiles did exist?

In answer, they had come up with several methods of dealing with the situation. All involved using Air Forces and smart bombs to destroy the missiles, launchers, support vehicles, electronics, and communication associated with them. No need to worry about the killing of technicians or support crews. The People's Republic would not complain. Nobody to complain to. Because no nation wanted another Communist power armed with missiles capable of carrying nuclear, chemical, or biological warheads in the region. Not even the wishy-washy United Nations would waffle over a new instance of weapons of mass destruction.

Once Zavello's staff had an OPLAN to submit to the Joint Chiefs, the one-eyed colonel ordered Swayne to look it over.

"Play the devil's asshole," Zavello said. "You're going to be the man on the ground, you and your team. What's wrong with this plan?"

Swayne scanned the options and handed it back.

"Don't tell me you can't find anything wrong," Zavello

said, baring the pointed ivory cones that lined his mouth, the teeth of a killer whale.

"With all due respect, Colonel—"

Zavello hissed at him, "Skip the shit, Captain."

"All right, sir, this plan is a disaster."

"How so? It's got everything a military officer needs to get the job done. Something in here you can't pull off? I can get somebody else, if you can't do the job." As he spoke, Zavello inclined his head forward like a drill instructor. If he had been wearing a drill instructor's hat over his slicked-back silver hair, he would have been pecking at Swayne's nose with its brim.

"Can you handle the truth? Sir?"

Zavello's face darkened at the reference to Jack Nicholson's fictional Marine colonel. "You're damned right I can. Give it to me."

Swayne tossed the OPLAN onto the colonel's desk. "This plan is written for a Force Recon team. Any team in the Marine Corps could carry it out. Trouble is, it's not written for the politicians who are going to have to approve it. It doesn't leave any wiggle room for anybody who wants to take the weasel's way out."

So the staff weenies rewrote the plan with an Alpha-One option directing the Spartans to destroy the missile in place and make it look like an accident.

Trouble was, once a unit in the field popped that first cap, touched off that first claymore, or directed that first artillery strike, all bets were off. Nobody knew where the stray bullets were going to fly. Nobody could calculate how an enemy would respond.

Nobody had guessed that Swayne would be faced with an extra man in the killing zone; for that matter, nobody could be all that sure the phantom man existed. All they had to confirm it was the word—make that the nose—of an indigenous man. Who even knew which side he was on? If the war in Afghanistan proved nothing else, it showed how quickly alliances, bargains, treasons, and betrayals could be shaped and reshaped among enemies, allies, friends, foes, and peaceniks. Nobody knew that better than Night Runner—Swayne had to detach him to the Army's Delta Force for two long months in Afghanistan.

All Swayne knew of the Montagnard he had learned after meeting him at their rally point inside Vietnam. Swayne made it an issue of survival never to jump into the same area where they were to meet somebody. No telling whether a traitor could arrange a greeting party, say, an infantry battalion. So he and his three men had dropped into a landing zone ten kilometers away from the rally point. They had met up with the Montagnard, one of the original people of the central highlands of Vietnam, Laos, and Cambodia long before those countries existed. *Montagnard* in French meant *mountaineer*.

Government after government had tried to incorporate the mountaineers into Vietnamese society. Assimilation was the name of that game. The Montagnards wanted no part of it. They had resisted, sometimes violently. They had been one of the most dependable American allies during the Vietnam War, mainly because they knew that the Communists would be the least likely to let them maintain their independent identity as a people. Like the rest of the country's allies, they, too, were abandoned in 1975. But that was history. This was now. Swayne stopped taking pictures of the raging fire. Mission complete. Time to get the hell out of Dodge.

SWAYNE GAVE ORDERS for everybody to gear up and stand by. With all the commotion going on down below, he saw no need for moving to a secondary rally point. They would hold in place until Night Runner and his companion joined them. Then they would clear the area, marching all night until they reached the nearest extraction point. They would say their thanks to their guide, pay him off in gold coins, and pull out of Vietnam once again.

At least that was the plan. Swayne knew how plans some-times went awry. Although, he did have to admit, this one had gone off almost perfectly. Hell, if it had not been for that self-imposed requirement to make the attack look like an accident, he would have had to call it flawless.

He saved those words in his memory bank. They would be good ones to use if Zavello got out of hand once he saw the pictures transmitted back to the OMCC.

He could hear the yelling already: *What the hell's with all the overkill? You couldn't just knock out the missile? You had to set all of Southeast Asia on fire?*

Zavello being Zavello, that's what he would bellow, his tirade salted with curses. Then he would dismiss Swayne and go report through the chain of command to the politicians that he had chewed out the officer in charge for causing all the ruckus "over there."

Even so, Zavello would have to agree, the whole thing went off pretty well. Swayne thought so up until the moment Night Runner returned, touching him on the shoulder before announcing himself, causing the startled Swayne nearly to jump out of both his position and his cammie underwear.

"Don't do that," Swayne said after he got his breathing under control. "Jeez, Runner, don't you ever worry about getting shot by one of your own?" In his night vision gog-gles, he saw a smart-aleck grin as Night Runner's gaze darted to the right, over Swayne's left shoulder.

"Where's—?" Swayne felt another touch on his shoulder. But at least this time he was tipped off by the movement of Night Runner's eyes, looking past him.

"—the Montagnard . . ." Swayne said, his voice trailing off.

Swayne turned to the bare-chested man and was shocked to see a third figure. The Montagnard pushed the Vietnamese soldier toward Swayne like a cat offering its master the gift of a wounded mouse. He recognized the sentry from below.

Swayne turned toward Night Runner. "You brought back a prisoner? Why?"

Night Runner recovered his pack and stood shrugging himself into it. "I'm sorry, Captain. I took off into the forest and had to keep running to stay ahead of the fire. When I finally connected with Monty here, he had a prisoner. I couldn't leave the man behind because of—"

"The goddamned accident thing," Swayne said, making it sound like the curse it was. If the sentry had survived the fire down below, he would be the one man able to tell his superiors that the destruction had been on purpose instead of an accident.

Night Runner shrugged. "Once we had a prisoner in our hands, alive and fairly healthy, there was nothing else to do but shoot him on the spot or bring him back with us." He checked the chamber of his ultralight 5.56 machine-gun, called the Brat for the sound it made when shooting at its highest rate of fire. He looked up from the gun. Swayne understood. They had talked about the things Runner had to do in the months he'd been detailed to the Army's Delta Force as part of a hunter-killer team in Afghanistan after the September 11 terrorist attacks. The things he'd done to terrorists he would not do to line soldiers, enemy or no, now that he'd rejoined his Force Recon team.

Swayne also got the point about the POW. He had seen the Montagnard carry the sentry away from the truck. At the time, it had seemed like a good idea. He couldn't very well be left dead on the side of the vehicle where he could be seen by the reaction force. Plus, there had been no way to lug him back down into the fire. The accident thing again, and now that the man was a prisoner, the Force Recon team could not murder him. Rather, Swayne *would not* murder him. No matter that it was the pragmatic thing to do. Swayne shook his head. Listening to his own thoughts, it seemed a fine distinction. Runner and the Montagnard had knowingly left several Vietnamese where they would be burned to grease spots. This man they had captured and somehow found it dishonorable to kill him. Instead, they would now handicap themselves, trying to escape through the forest, dragging an anchor. Once they got to the extraction point, what then?

If they turned the guy over to the Montagnard, Swayne knew well enough what would happen. The sentry would die as soon as the helicopter was out of sight. Nobody would ever accuse Swayne directly of being an accessory before the fact of murder. But he would know it. Hell, he had half a mind—

A smile creased his face. No, he had more than half a mind to do it. He would extract the Vietnamese sentry with them. Take the guy back to America. Turn him over to the chairborne commandos. They had demanded an accident. Let them deal with its fallout.

He realized that Night Runner was still waiting for orders. "We take him with us," he said. "We've already spent too much time here. Let's saddle up and clear the area. Greiner, get over here."

When the corporal came hustling out of the darkness into Swayne's field of night vision, he knew what his mission would be. "You want me to take charge of the EPW, sir?"

"Right. Charlie here belongs to you. Make sure his hands are secured."

"Charlie, sir? You know the enemy prisoner of war's name?"

Swayne had to laugh. "Charlie it is. I'll explain later."

They marched away from the dying orange glow behind them. Charlie. The name brought back all that he had read about the enemy during the war of his father—and he had read a lot. The Vietcong, VC, for short. Victor Charlie when saying the letters VC over the radio. GIs, who created a language for every war, called them Charlie in the Vietnam

War. Charlie was the enemy then, and he was the enemy now.

No, the Vietnamese sentry was not Vietcong. The VC had been irregulars during the war from 1963 to 1975. They were South Vietnamese guerrilla fighters, allies of the People's Army of Vietnam, the PAVN, commonly called the North Vietnamese Army, NVA. Both the VC and NVA had fought against the Americans and Army of Vietnam, ARVN. Quite possibly, this youngster would not even know what any of the terms meant.

Now that the two Vietnams had long been united, everybody in uniform was a PAVN. Swayne considered every PAVN his enemy, including this simple soldier. The Vietcong, the North Vietnamese Army regulars, the NVA, the PAVN: all enemies. The ones with the older names had killed his father in this country. They had not turned over his remains after the truce. They had played head games with American politicians. And they had played body games with his father, denying that he had ever existed, crossing his name off the list of missing in action or possible prisoners of war. Just like that. A slash of a black pen, and his father did not exist, except as a Marine officer sent to Vietnam.

Sorry, Charlie, thought Swayne. *Not that easy. Time for payback.* Starting with the enemy soldier. Swayne adjusted his night vision binoculars. No matter that this Charlie wasn't born until ten years after the war ended. Sometimes sons had to pay for the sins of the fathers.

Not that it mattered. Their duty done, Team Midnight would soon be winging their way out of Vietnam. Swayne felt a twinge of regret. He would have liked to stay a few days longer. Get the feel of the country where his father went missing. Get a sense for the days and nights in the land where his father had died. Get in touch with a life he did not remember by reflecting on loss and death, perhaps even imprisonment and torture. Get a taste of this little piece of hell on earth.

THE REFUELING SITE
0414 HOURS LOCAL

HALFWAY TO HELL, buried deep in darkness, a pair of eyes stared upward, waiting for the earth to stop burning.

Only after Nguyen tat Thant could no longer hear the roar of flames consuming the fuel depot, the camp, the truck, the forest, and his men, did he open his eyes. Only when he could no longer see the flicker of fire did he think he might have the barest chance to survive.

Even then he dared not call out. Nobody up on earth above him would be able to help him. The only people alive would be those who had tried to kill him. They would not help. They would only finish him.

Tat Thant had made this run with the precious cargo of missiles three times before already, one missile at a time. Even so, he had not treated any of his trips as routine. He had dispersed his forces ahead on the road and behind the missile. He had left two men with the truck. Each time he had awakened the small security force at the depot's refueling station before posting the road ahead and behind the missile carrier.

He would never take his mission for granted, not if he had made the run a hundred times. His country had entrusted him with the security of a strategic defense missile, one that could well make the People's Republic a world power, his superiors had told him. He understood and believed what they said.

Yet somehow he had failed in his mission. An enemy force of terrorists had struck the country at its heart. They had destroyed part of that strategic defense system, killing perhaps forty soldiers, the flower of Vietnam's youth. Indeed, the enemy had destroyed part of Vietnam itself. It was as if he had witnessed a return of the fabled huge bombers that left strings of enormous potholes across the landscape, the B-52s. Of all the stories he had heard about that war, none were more frightening or more vivid than hushed tales of the ear-splitting chains of explosions that wrenched the earth, leveled the forests, and made eardrums and even bodies burst.

At the first sound of the alarm, he had roused his soldiers and rallied them, ordering them over the radio to return at once to the truck from both directions. He had called to the fuel depot's security force, but nobody had answered the radio. Either the men had gone back to sleep, or the terrorists had killed them at their posts. Then, when his force had returned to the missile carrier to counterattack, the enemy had set Vietnam on fire.

These things he rehearsed as he tried to save himself. He would need to recall the exact words, sequences, and times when making his report. He needed to focus on every detail of the night, so he could put together the picture for the regiment of investigators who would come here to look into the attack. He would make his report thorough and precise. The longer the report, the longer they would let him live. Then, because surely he was the only one to survive this vicious, cowardly attack, his superiors would execute him.

He had acted properly, according to his instructions and his best instincts. But both had failed him. He had positioned his noncommissioned officer with the security force at the tail of the formation. He had received assurances that the rear guard had deployed into the forest, the truck parked across the road so that no enemy force could attack the missile carrier down the road from behind. He had received reports every ten minutes on the march, every five minutes at halt. He had roused the ten-man security force at the depot, giving a tongue-lashing to the junior officer in charge of securing the site. Not so much that the young man had done anything wrong. More to instill fear enough that he would not suffer a lapse in judgment.

Then, within seconds of learning that something had gone wrong with the walking guard, he had called on his radio to the stationary guard inside the truck. Without even waiting for a response, he had ordered both security details into action. They had reached the carrier within two minutes.

Just in time, he recalled, feeling a deep sadness in his heart, for the fiery explosions that had killed his men. Explosions that should have killed him, too. He wished now that he had died in the fire. Better that than to suffer the retribution of his country. Not so much because of the pain that he would have to bear. There would be that, of course. He could live with that. But to shame his family and betray his country in a moment was too much.

Far better to have died in battle.

Still, at the moment of the explosions, when flames had streaked through the sky, trying to cover him with a net of fire, he had thought of nothing but survival. When his clothes began to burn, when his head was enveloped by the smoke of his own burning hair, when he looked behind him and saw a tidal wave of fiery fuel boiling toward him, he never once gave a thought to giving in to it. He had run. Toward the water well. He had leaped over the stone wall and into the well. He had slid down the rope, feeling the burn on his hands to go along with that on his head and his back. Until finally he'd dropped the rope, caught the bucket between his legs, and fell into the water at the bottom.

The shock of the cold on the scorching spots of his body had nearly killed him as he inhaled water. For a second, coughing and choking, he felt ready to give up. Above his head an orange circle of light was all that he could see. He could not tell whether the flames were burning on top of the water or in the sky. He did not try to swim to the surface. Not at first. He told himself it would be better to drown than to burn.

But he could not allow it to happen, either. Desperate for air, he broke the surface to find the air clean and cold. He would have to die another way. In shame. He would try to endure the disgrace. He would ask for only one punishment. He would beg his superiors to arm him with a rifle so that he could go after the terrorists that had caused so much harm to his country, so much shame to his family, his father most of all, his father a hero of the war against America.

For an hour, he floated on the surface of the well, holding the water bucket upside down, trapping air, allowing it to buoy him. The only sounds were the roar of the flames and the rattling of thin gunfire, which, he decided, was not a gunfight but rifle and machine gun rounds exploding in the fire. Then the pain of his burns at the back of his head and on his palms forced him inside himself. He hugged the bucket, closing his eyes, trying to keep his focus as the chills set in.

He promised himself. He would get out of this well. He would explain things to his superiors. Surely they would let him go after his enemy.

When it came time to climb out into the blackness above, he started up the rope, climbing, feeling the pain in his raw palms, letting it focus his hatred. The smoldering rope broke, sending him back into the well.

Tat Thant accepted that fate, too. He deserved it. It was just more of the punishment allotted to him. He would have to find another way out of the well.

Floating on his back in the cramped space, he doubled his body up, putting his feet against one side of the well. Using his shoulder blades, scorched though they were, as the ribs of the python, he began inching upward, keeping himself pressed between the two walls. Inch by inch he lifted himself free of the water. In an hour, he could no longer hear water from his clothing dripping into the surface of the well. Above him, he could not see the sky, it was still so dark.

His legs cramped. His back throbbed. Getting a breath was

difficult. At first he thought his problem was merely being cramped in the space. Then he realized that his throat hurt. He might have inhaled the flames, burning his lungs.

Just one more reason to go after his enemy. Just one more justification for killing them, as many as there were, as painfully as he could. Even so, nothing would be more painful than when his father learned that his son had let down their country.

WITH LITTLE MORE than an hour to go before morning nautical twilight, Swayne purged his mind of efforts to resurrect his father. And gladly. He had been too young. He had seen all the war movies about all the wars, especially the semi-realistic ones—*Apocalypse Now, Platoon, The Thin Red Line*—as well as the too-realistic ones—*Saving Private Ryan, Blackhawk Down, We Were Soldiers*.

Even reading every book about Vietnam could not give him a feel for that war. He had been in battle, so he had always thought that if he could only visit, he would get the sense of his father's war. Now that he was here, he still couldn't put it together. He supposed the problem was not so much that he could not get a grip on the war. He couldn't get a grip on his father. That was the problem. His uncles had treated him like a nephew. His grandfather had treated him like a stepson. Nobody had treated him like a son, except for his father, and Swayne's only recollections were dim and fleeting and likely wrong, too.

Now that they were within five minutes of being picked up by a stealth helicopter, he didn't have space for his father in his mind. So he lovingly put him away in his place in his heart.

The team moved into a tight perimeter at the edge of the forest. About fifty meters away was the spot where a helicopter would come in. Night Runner had gone out already; he had put down a personal locater beacon set to a prearranged frequency. A transponder inside the helicopter would send out an interrogation signal. Until it received a signal, the PERLOBE would remain silent; that was a new feature added since they had lost a PERLOBE to the enemy several missions ago. Now the team hardly used them, except when interrogated by the electronic handshake. This one would send out a five-second signal, giving the pilot an opportunity to set up the proper heading. The transponder would calculate the distance to PERLOBE's position by comparing the aircraft's GPS position to that of the PERLOBE, as determined by the overhead satellite. Inside the cockpit, the pilot would be flying using a night vision system so clear that he could fly to the spot in total blackout, landing with the PERLOBE under the nose of the aircraft as easily if it were broad daylight with flashing streamers and smoke signals on the ground to guide him. Once the craft began its descent to landing, the team would hustle to the pickup site. The aircraft would not be on the ground more than ten seconds.

Swayne had already given instructions for boarding in the premission briefing. Since things had changed, he ordered Friel and Greiner to take the prisoner aboard and secure him, so he could not jump out, or worse, jump the pilots. Greiner gave him a roger, and Friel only hesitated a second, grunted once, and said, "Wilco." Swayne picked up on the pause. For a second, he thought the old Friel had returned. The old Friel would have complained about having to pull guard duty on a single gook, when he should have been setting up to take on an entire enemy regiment.

Night Runner would be the last on board, after collecting the locator beacon. Swayne would express his thanks to the Montagnard and hand over a leather pouch filled with six ounces of pure gold, six Krugerrands.

Once on board, Swayne would keep his eye on the Montagnard as Night Runner mounted up. On takeoff, they would not trust the guide. If he even took his rifle off his shoulder, Night Runner and Swayne would train their sights on his body, their weapons set to full auto. If he raised his weapon toward the aircraft, he would die a rich man, his pouch full of gold, his body rotting away on the LZ.

Swayne set his own personal locator beacon to the same frequency as the one in the landing zone, making sure his transmitter was off. He could receive the aircraft signal without sending a contradictory response. His own beacon would do the math for him, telling him how far away the aircraft was at each interrogation signal. No words would have to be exchanged.

Almost as soon as he said it, the beacon, the size of a credit card and thick as four cards stacked, began to vibrate. A tiny LED screen lit up, no brighter than the face of his wristwatch, showing him an arrow, an azimuth readout, and a distance. Twenty kilometers away at 275 degrees true, almost due west.

Before he could give instructions to his team, a familiar voice came over the radio. Zavello.

"Spartan One this is Eagle One, stand by for a change of mission."

"Wilco." *Now what?* What new scheme had the harebrained desk jockeys invented? Why didn't Zavello tell him an hour ago that a change was in the works? For that matter, why hadn't somebody told the helicopter pilot, so he did not have to risk his ass flying in here?

As he waited for orders, he expected to see the helicopter to peel off and return back to Thailand. It did not. He started to get antsy. He wanted to get on the radio and tell the OMCC that he had a prisoner to send back. On the other hand, he didn't want anybody to know he had the captive yet. Didn't want them to give him orders to leave the Vietnamese behind. He wanted to deliver the man and let them deal with the problem. He felt a moment of shame as he realized that he was thinking like Friel. But, what the hell? Why not enjoy one moment of the dark, secret pleasures? It might give him an insight into Friel.

His PERLOBE buzzed again. The aircraft had set up on

final approach to landing. *Why not?* If the pilots didn't know any better, what would prevent him from going out to meet the craft and strapping the Vietnamese soldier in before letting it return to base?

A smile creased his lips.

He crossed the tiny perimeter and made a snipping to motion with his fingers in front of Night Runner's eyes. They both shut off their microphones. Swayne told Runner his plan. Together, they took their prisoner out toward the beacon on the LZ. The aircraft was just thirty seconds out, and Swayne could hear the stealth craft's muffled blades snicking through the air. All the way out to the landing zone, he could not wipe the smile off his face.

The aircraft came in low and hot, skimming the trees at the edge of the clearing, flaring abruptly, its tail wheel dropping dangerously close to the forest before the craft leveled out and settled over the spot where they had placed the beacon, its front wheels straddling the device. By instinct, Swayne lowered his head and ran toward the craft. But before he had even approached close enough to be covered by the rotor disk, he felt a sudden blast. The blades bit into the air, and the craft screwed itself upward, into the darkness.

Swayne, holding the right elbow of their prisoner in his left hand, and his rifle in his right, stared upward, watching the craft vanish over the treetops. The smile on his face now felt like the stupid grin it was. He was glad for the darkness. One thing to smile and be a villain. Quite another to smile and be a jackass.

A familiar voice called to him from the OMCC. "Spartan One this is Eagle One, over."

"This is Spartan One, over."

Zavello. He had probably just finished talking to the helicopter pilots on their aviation frequency, telling them to clear the landing zone, after all. Now he would have the change of mission for—

"Swayne? Is that you?"

Swayne had never heard Zavello talk so informally on the radio. Except for his occasional fits of swearing. Besides, he should know who was on the radio. Didn't the old man recognize his voice by now?

"Roger, standing by for the change in mission."

All at once he felt a tug from the Vietnamese soldier, folding up for a fall.

"Down." Night Runner said.

Swayne didn't wait for an explanation. He dropped to a knee, the POW lying beside him. Then he saw it: the figure not twenty feet away, standing in the LZ.

"What the hell are you three doing?"

Swayne's ears and eyes would not reconcile the image with his brain. The voice was Zavello's. The figure's was, too. One man, tall, bulky, wearing Marine Corps tactical gear, including a set of high-tech night vision goggles with binocular vision capability. Standing in the LZ.

Swayne looked over the outstretched body of their prisoner toward Night Runner. The gunny stared at him, his jaw slack, mouth open. It had to be. *Zavello*? *Here*?

Swayne heard the crackling of dry vegetation, interpreted the phantom's swagger as a Marine, recognized the jungle pattern of Force Recon cammies, saw the weapons of a Marine. Clearly a Marine. That smile of sneering, wicked, uneven teeth. It had to be. Zavello. A tiny hope tried to wriggle out of the darkness that cloaked Swayne's soul. The binocular goggles. Surely that meant two eyes.

The figure lifted up the hinged lenses. Swayne saw the eye-patch.

"Shit," he hissed. One eye.

"Is that any way to greet your commanding officer?" Zavello growled, his grin gaping to expose rounded, pointed teeth of the Orca on the attack.

Night Runner, always the one with quicker instincts, got to his feet first and found an excuse to get clear of the line of fire.

"I'll collect the beacon," he said.

"Take the prisoner with you." Swayne didn't want the man around. He wasn't so much worried about an enemy hearing tactical intel. He just didn't want another human being to witness to his senior captor's ass-chewing. Not even if the man didn't understand the English curse words.

Zavello waited for Night Runner and the Vietnamese sentry to get clear of their hearing. He fiddled with his microphone. "Where's the switch? The one you use to shut these things off every time you want to keep me from listening in when you want to call me names behind my back?"

"Yes, sir." By now Swayne had gotten over his shock. He could tell Zavello was only faking a bitter mood. He reached across the darkness, found the microphone switch at the man's ear, and shut it off.

"I thought I told you to stand by for a change in mission."

"Yes, sir."

Zavello laughed, making the sound of a squealing fan belt. "Hoo-boy, this trip is quite an eye-opener. Amazing the things you can see in only ten seconds on the ground, things you never see from the OMCC."

"Sir?"

"Where did you ever get the idea that standing by meant jumping on a helicopter? What were you doing? Going for a joyride?"

"No, sir."

"Making a beer run?"

"No, sir."

"Whore run, then?"

"No, sir. We were putting the prisoner on the craft."

"The prisoner, yes, the prisoner." Zavello was toying with him. He had seen the prisoner, had heard Swayne tell Night Runner to guard him. "I don't remember anybody saying anything about a prisoner. Do you remember anybody saying anything about a prisoner?" Clearly, he was enjoying himself, addressing Swayne as if he were in a town meeting on the campaign trail in Iowa instead of standing in a jungle clearing in a country where anybody with a weapon would kill him on sight. He took a deep breath and puffed out his barrel chest. "Was this unreported prisoner going to attempt an escape from ten thousand feet?"

Swayne turned his head, pressed his thumb against one nostril, and blew a stream of steam out the other. Enough, already. The old man was having a good time. Swayne didn't think it was funny anymore. He answered in measured tones. Not enough to be insubordinate. But not hiding his anger, either.

"I decided to send the Vietnamese back to Washington. Let the people who wanted Force Recon to pull off this mission and make it look like an accident realize that this is not a game. It's not the movies. It's life. It's death. Let them deal with this Vietnamese. I wasn't going to kill him or let him be killed. Let them take responsibility for the mess they helped create. That's what I was doing. Sir."

Swayne's thinly veiled anger wasn't going to ruin Zavello's good mood.

"There it is then. Take me to your Montagnard."

TAT THANT KNEW that he was nearing the top of the well when he could feel the slight, cold breeze blowing across his face. Even so, the air did not refresh him. The scent of diesel fuel poisoned every breath. He felt that at any second a stray spark would reignite the fumes. An explosion would finish him off finally, perhaps dropping him back down inside the well. There he would poison the water as he rotted. For a moment, he thought he might welcome it. Perhaps reach into his pocket, produce his cigarette lighter, and touch off the atmosphere himself. If only he could be assured that it would kill him. That it would not just increase or prolong the torture of the nerves burned raw on his back and head. If only he would not find himself wanting to climb out of the well once more, a feat he could never repeat.

Then he remembered why he wanted out of this well in the first place. To punish the saboteurs who had disgraced him. He told himself to be realistic. After all, it was not patriotism that drove him. He had to admit it. It was the personal nature of the attack, the attempt to embarrass him before his nation. His father had risen to the rank of colonel, a regimental commander in the People's Army. Now in partial retirement as commander of a labor camp, he would be shamed when he heard that one of his nation's strategic weapons, one under the care of his own son, had been destroyed.

Reason enough to stay alive. Simply to avenge himself and justify the name of his disgraced father, who would not even know that he was disgraced until the morning sun rose and shed its light on the disaster outside this well.

With that incentive, tat Thant finally grasped the edge of the three-foot wall that topped the well. With one final supreme effort, he hauled himself up. His trembling legs had nothing left. He could not even lift one over the wall. He simply lunged like a breaching whale, throwing himself over the top, landing on the warm, wet, oily earth.

He felt as if he might pass out. The smell of fumes was so strong, even if something did not set off a spark, the fumes might suffocate him by starving his lungs of oxygen. So, one limb at a time, he got himself to his hands and knees and began crawling.

One hand, then one knee. Then the other hand and the other knee. He inched along. Nothing automatic about it. He had to remind himself which hand to move, which knee. He had to keep track of the order. If he did not, he might fall on his face again after a knee bashed into an elbow, buckling his arm, dumping him on his face. Even at that, he fell twice. The taste of diesel in his mouth revived his disgust. He had climbed out of the well. Now was not the time to die. He kept going. Until, at last, he saw the pinpoint of a light ahead of him.

No, a fire. Perhaps a piece of kindling still burning in the forest. He decided not to go that way after all.

Then he heard a voice. A small laugh came to him from the fire.

He sat back on his haunches, then worked his hands up his thighs to his waist so he could kneel erect. He cupped his hands behind his ears, finding to his horror that he had no ears. Except for two short lumps of cartilage next to his neck, they had been burned off. Funny, that. He had not even felt them missing until now.

Another reason for anger at the terrorists. Even now, they might be preparing to ambush the military unit that would eventually respond to this attack. For surely, somebody had reported the fire by now. Somebody had tried to contact him on the radio. Hearing no response, they would have sent a reaction force, the regiment standing by to the south.

The idea of an enemy nearby revived him. He found strength to struggle to his feet. Once standing, he realized he was barely dressed. His pants had burned off from behind, and only a clump of rags hung from his belt at his waist. He reached behind him to discover that his legs were bare and wet with his own ooze. He touched his head and began to weep. He had been proud of his beautiful mop, so black it lay like a blue sheen capping his head. Now there was nothing except woolly clumps. Bare patches of his scalp had swollen with liquid, giving him blisters the size and feel of shucked oysters.

Terrorists had done this to him. Now he must get his revenge. He looked around him for weapon and could not find one. To his left he saw a low, angular shape, burning at each of its four corners. The truck of the rear security force, its tires on fire. He went to it. In the back were at least three bodies lying together in a heap of half-cooked flesh. There might have been more, but he could not tell. The smell of charred flesh did not bother him as much as he thought it would. Perhaps because he had taken that smell into the well with himself.

He did see a rifle inside the back of the truck, a Kalashnikov. But the wood stock still glowed like a chunk of charcoal in a cooking pit. He was certain that the weapon had been too damaged by fire to shoot. In any case, all the ammunition in the truck would have already cooked off in the first half hour of the fire.

Inside the cab of the truck, the driver still sat upright, the skeleton of his left hand and forearm welded to the steering wheel, his right still on the gear of shift lever. From what tat Thant could see in the flickering light, the hand had pushed the lever into reverse. The man had been trying to back away from the tidal wave of fire when he had been hit.

Tat Thant reached for the door handle of the truck, but the searing heat radiating to the palm of his bleeding hand stopped him short. The bare flesh on his palm hurt enough already. No sense in punishing himself by grilling the open wound.

He caught a glimpse of movement to his left and prepared to leap at it. It was his reflection in a fragment of the truck's mirror, cracked and crazed by the heat. He did not dare to look for more than a single, fleeting second. It was enough. The eerie glow made it seem as if his head had been made of wax and put too near the hearth. His ears had already melted away, his hair, except for an untouched shock of bangs, had gone up in smoke. An area from his hairline to his chin in depth and from one cheek to the other in width had been spared. The rest of his flesh had begun to slough off.

One glance and one moment of reflection told him all he needed to know. He was as good as dead. Already his lungs had begun to fill up. A good deal of his skin had peeled away, which would make him subject to oxygen starvation, eventually shock, and finally infection, although he doubted he would live long enough to die from that.

He might have enough strength left for a couple hours of life. He shook his head in disgust. If only he had not been forced to use up so much energy climbing out of the well.

He stumbled away from the mirror and nearly tripped over something in the roadway. From the sound of it as he kicked it, a sound muted because of his impaired hearing, he realized that it was a rifle. He bent over and found it in the shadows of the ruts. Still warm to the touch, it hurt his raw hands, but it did not scorch him. A quick examination using his fingertips told him the magazine had exploded as the ammunition blew up. It was an AK-50, a carbine version of the AK-47. Because it had no wood stock but instead a telescoping metal stock, it had cooled off more quickly. He found the hinged bayonet intact and fumbled to release the catch that kept it folded beneath the barrel. Once he had fully extended the bayonet, he was satisfied. At last, a weapon.

He turned toward the flicker of the firelight in the forest and crept through the brittle ashes of the woods toward the foliage beyond the burn.

He was too unsteady to remain surefooted. Even so, he realized, it was not necessary to sneak. The voices of the men he intended to kill were loud enough to drown out the sound of his own footsteps. They were laughing. Probably celebrating their victory. He would snatch that victory from them. Show them defeat. Kill as many as he could before they killed him.

It would be a small enough measure of revenge, but it would have to do. He had no more to give than his life.

ZAVELLO WOULD HAVE been content to conduct his briefing inside the forest just at the edge of the landing zone. Swayne would not allow it.

"We have to clear the area," he said. "Because of the helicopter. If anybody spotted it, they will come. Or else they will shoot artillery."

Zavello shook his head. "I've been behind a desk for too

long," he murmured, as much to himself as anybody on the team. It was as close to an apology as he would ever allow himself. Swayne knew that the colonel had once been in the infantry himself. So he would remember the tactic, drilled into his head in his own war in this country more than a quarter century ago. Clear the LZ, dammit, clear the LZ.

Swayne gave the order. Night Runner, the Montagnard, and he would lead out. Greiner would follow with the captive, then Zavello, with Friel bringing up the rear guard.

Even so, Zavello wasn't finished. "I want to meet your Montagnard. The one called Monty?"

Swayne shrugged. "That's what he calls himself."

"Monty? You there?"

Zavello spoke the name so loudly that Night Runner cringed, Friel snickered, and Swayne nearly told him to shut up. The old man was fast becoming the kind of pain in the ass that Friel used to be.

"Tin-Tin Zavello? Surely you shit."

The tall, flat figure came out of the darkness. Zavello flipped up his goggles so his one-eyed vision could not be deceived. Without another word, the two men went at each other and hugged like brothers, repeating to each other, "Surely you shit." They broke apart and spoke to each other in French, hugged again, and broke apart.

Zavello growled at Swayne. "What the hell are you waiting for, Captain? I thought you said we were going to clear the area."

Stunned, Swayne had nothing to say. He turned to Night Runner, and they exchanged quick, small wags of their heads. Then Night Runner wheeled on a heel and headed out to a rally point, taking a roundabout route to a spot that the team had picked in case this landing zone was compromised. Zavello moved up behind Night Runner, having decided to walk beside his Montagnard friend, a living, breathing relic of his own war.

Swayne fell into march position behind them. He wasn't

about to say anything that might inspire Zavello to take command of the team. The colonel was capable of anything. Swayne had always admired him for his ability not to interfere over the radio during operations on the ground. Now he did not know what to think. The man had joined the operation. Swayne still did not even know why. He would not find out until they reached the rally point and he could get a briefing.

Even so, Zavello still had surprises in store for him. Before they had marched a hundred meters, the Montagnard reached over and grasped the colonel's hand. They marched hand in hand like girlfriends through the forest, separating for the trees and rejoining hands afterward.

Swayne did not even know what to feel, except for the prickles of shame for his superior officer.

Friel didn't mind letting his opinion be known, though. He coughed a fake cough twice, like a man getting checked for a hernia.

Zavello released the Montagnard's hand to turn on his microphone, then spoke so loudly, the radio wasn't necessary.

"In this part of the world, it's an act of friendship, of brotherhood, of family. You wouldn't understand it, Sergeant Friel."

Zavello's tone cured Friel's cough.

FINALLY, TAT THANT drew close enough to the fire to see that this was not an ambush. The soldiers were not terrorists at all, but his own men. Six of them crowded close to the fire to brew tea and boil rice. The six sat laughing and joking; from the looks on their faces. His poor knobs of ears did not allow him to hear their precise words, although he could hear the singsong of his language.

As he sneaked through the forest, he carried the assault rifle, bayonet fixed, at port arms. He had screwed up his courage. He was ready to dash into the midst of his enemy, no matter how many there were, ready to stab and plunge and kill, until somebody killed him. Now, disappointed, he tried to drop the useless gun on the forest floor so he could walk into the circle of firelight unarmed.

But when he released his grip, the gun would not fall from his palms. His blood had glued the weapon to his flesh. He tried to pull his left hand free, but the pain was too much.

So, tears in his eyes, his clothing hanging like black charred rags, his blackened weapon held at the ready across his chest, he staggered out of the forest and into the tiny clearing beneath the canopy where his men sat around the fire.

He might as well have thrown a hand grenade into their midst. Two of the men saw him at once, screamed, and dove for their weapons. Two others ran into the jungle, shouting a warning. One soldier, his sergeant, held a bowl to his lips, a scoop of rice suspended before the gaping hole of his mouth. The sixth man pulled up his weapon and began firing on automatic at the apparition, the blister that had grown legs and arms and walked up on them. The man cursed at him, calling him a monster, a ghost, a demon. An entire magazine from his AK-47 sprayed the ground at tat Thant's feet, hit the greenery behind him, and one bullet nicked the bayonet and stung his fingers.

At that, tat Thant shrieked, adding one more dimension of terror to the scene in the forest. Somehow the soldier with the rifle had missed him. Tat Thant cried out, "Stop shooting, you fool."

The man shouted, "Monster! Monster!" He pulled a second magazine and tried to load it on top of the first thirty-round clip. Finally he came to his senses enough to know he had to eject the expended clip first. He did. He inserted the second one and began to raise the rifle, began to shoot again, trying to kill his commanding officer, shooting low, the recoil of the rifle forcing the muzzle to rise.

Again, he failed. He fell over onto his back, the Kalashnikov firing into the sky, the weapon clenched in his grip as he died, a nicked, burnt, bayonet run through his chest, pinning him to the ground.

"Captain?" It was tat Thant's noncommissioned officer speaking over his bowl of rice.

"Yes."

"Are you all right?"

"A stupid question, wouldn't you say, Sergeant? What does it look like?"

The sergeant was looking at his officer's back. He could see vertebrae sticking out of the skin, and a pair of ribs that had been rubbed to the bone from the climb out of the well. He had seen roasted pigs on rotating spits that looked less well done than his commander.

"Sir, you look as if—"

"Forget it, Sergeant. I know what I look like. Gather the men. If you please, make certain that nobody else tries to kill me. Then come here and help me get this rifle free of my hands."

NIGHT RUNNER FOUND a deep thicket not far from the clearing. The canopy overhead was so thick that the dawn could not find its way into the spot for almost an hour after the team had occupied it, although the clearing had grown bright. A steep ravine ran through the middle of the thicket, and a trickle of water rattled, making the sight and sound of glass rosary beads over black pebbles at the bottom.

Zavello volunteered to take custody of the Vietnamese prisoner. Greiner would not give him up until he got permission from his captain. He looked his way, and Swayne gave it with a nod of his head. Zavello smirked but did not say anything. He was willing to grant Swayne command of the field operation for now. Swayne doubted it could last.

Zavello and the Montagnard worked their way down the ravine, stepping from boulder to boulder. Once at the bottom, they propped their Vietnamese prisoner against the wall of the ravine. They sat side by side on a boulder of the size of a coffee table, arms draped over each other's shoulders like a teenage couple at a drive-in movie. They chattered like kids, alternating among Zavello's halting Vietnamese, the Montagnard's halting English, and French, which Zavello managed well enough.

Swayne organized the position, putting Greiner just inside the thicket, where he could look over their back trail. He directed Night Runner and Friel to shut off their microphones, so he could talk to them.

"That's a relief," said Friel, yanking the receiver free of his ear. "Sounds like a couple old ladies on speed."

"Henry," said Night Runner, "the man might hear you."

"I don't care if he does."

Night Runner and Swayne both stared at him.

"Right," Friel said. "I do care. Last thing I want is that man yelling in my face. You've ever smell how bad his breath is? I've had toilet-licking dogs—"

"Henry," said Swayne, covering his microphone. "My mike is still hot."

Friel's eyes widened. He gripped his weapon, as if he might have to fight to save his own life. Swayne and Night Runner winked at each other. Friel caught it.

"Captain, you hadn't ought to do that. Only underwear I got is on me already. And now they're ruined."

They all listened to Zavello and Monty for a few seconds, until Friel added his last word on the topic, which reassured Swayne that the kid was getting back to normal. "Somebody ought to tell the man his mike is hot." Friel looked from Swayne to Night Runner.

Night Runner said, "That sounds like a good job for the junior sergeant on the team."

Friel thought it over for a nanosecond as the voice boomed out of the ravine. "Belay my last. Somebody ought to tell the man to shut off his bullhorn."

Night Runner grew serious. "What next, Captain?"

Swayne shook his head, his mouth forming the answer,

Who knows? He had never been on a tactical mission where they had time to joke around. They had always had a secondary mission, a target, an enemy to find or to hide from.

"You two get some rest," he said. "I'll wait until the old man gets a notion to tell me what's on his mind. In four hours or so you can spell Greiner and me. Maybe I will know something by then."

"He's going to talk for four hours?" Friel said.

Swayne ignored it. He moved to the opposite side of the thicket so he could watch over the clearing and the jungle beyond. Night Runner came by and whispered that he would be making a circuit of the position to see whether any trails, game or human, might put them in danger from a wandering patrol.

Swayne appreciated the thought, something he wished had occurred to him. Already Zavello was having his effect on him, a negative effect. He found a place to sit against the tree, but he would not allow himself to get comfortable. It was an old trick. If he fell asleep, he would topple and awaken. Or the leg bent beneath him would begin to throb in half an hour, and he would have to change positions, putting some other part of his body in pain. He could do the four hours of staying awake on his head. In fact, that might be another position to consider, he told himself. Any other day he might have smiled at the thought. Not today. To his mind, they had not moved far enough away from the spot where they had struck the truck.

After an hour, Swayne repositioned himself. The conversation inside the ravine had not let up. He had been forced to turn down his volume as Zavello and the Montagnard talked and laughed. They were obnoxious enough so Swayne knew he need not worry about falling asleep.

Swayne learned from their snatches of conversation that the two had served together during the Vietnam War in a long-range recon unit. From that he got the idea that Zavello might have been one of the first officers in Force Recon, or

at least in units that would later become the basis for the
Force Recon concept. The Montagnard had guided Marines
on some missions. Clearly, they had gotten into several
scrapes together. Zavello had been wounded inside Laos
while fighting with the Montagnard. Zavello, then a lieutenant, had directed B-52 strikes. Swayne shuddered at that.
The idea of giving bombing coordinates to a pilot flying
five miles up did not suit him. Neither did being on the
ground when the B-52 dropped a bellyful of half-ton bombs
in free fall. Zavello was lucky that he had lost only an eye
to combat.

TAT THANT FELT that he had finally gotten a stroke of good
luck. One of his men had had the uncommon good sense to
run away from the truck with the medical kit. In it were
enough drugs to ease his pain. His man wanted to fully se-
date him, but he insisted on staying alert. He asked them to
dress his wounds. They did their best, wrapping him like a
mummy with bandages from top to bottom after applying
ointments and disinfectants from the medical kit. Nobody
knew for sure what the medicines were supposed to do for
such radical wounds. They just did what their captain told
them to do. Once he had been covered from neck to toe in
bandages, the men began looking in their packs for the larg-
est jacket and trousers for him to wear over the bandages.
He ordered them to give him the holster, belt, and pistol from
the junior lieutenant he had stabbed with the bayonet.

One man saw that tat Thant was losing fluids as fast as a
canvas water bag. Already the bandages had soaked through
in the back, and his clothing was plastered to his body, as if
he had laid down in a puddle of glue. His noncommissioned
officer suggested that he start drinking water and chewing
salt tablets so he would not become dehydrated. Half of his
men avoided looking at him, he was such a sight from the
neck up, with sores and blisters except for his face; the other

half would only look him in the eyes, the least damaged area of his visible body.

Tat Thant gave instructions that nobody was to answer the radio. Not that it mattered, because nobody had one, it turned out. He told the men that they would be going after the enemy who had done this to them. He said that they would have to move quickly, for he had not much strength. He doubted he could survive past today to get the mission done, but did not say so.

The five men looked at each other and then at him.

The NCO spoke for them: "We should get medical attention for you, Captain. Don't you think we should make our report and wait for reinforcements?"

"Neither. We will go after our enemy, the terrorists."

One of his men, made bold by the captain's weak voice and apparent deafness, said, "I'm not going out there. Who knows how many the enemy are?"

Tat Thant drew his newly acquired pistol from its holster and shot the man twice in the chest. The remaining four soldiers stepped back in horror. "He was correct. He is not going with us. Is there anyone else so bold as to make a similar prediction?" When nobody spoke up, the captain put his pistol away.

After a stark minute of silence, tat Thant yanked his canteen from his belt. His men cringed until they saw that he had not drawn his pistol again. *Good.* A little fear would make them wary. He pulled at the tepid water, filling his belly. An eddy of air swept across his skull, and he felt its chill through to the core of his body. For a moment, he smiled at the thought the water he'd just drunk had poured out his back. His smile reflected in the face of his men as a new horror. He wondered that his smile did not set them to flight. His face, the only healthy part of his body they could see, must look as odd as an omelet on a dung pile. He dug in his first aid packet and withdrew a pair of salt tablets. He crushed them between his teeth and washed them down with more water from his canteen. He cringed at the stinging on the palm of his hand from the salt. Then he drank another half canteen and ordered everybody to fill theirs before they struck out. "Drink as much water as you can," he ordered. "Drink more than you can hold, until you're ready to burst. Half of all that you carry into the forest, I will have to drink. Do this for me, and I will reward you in whatever way I can."

He looked to his NCO. "You were once a woodsman, weren't you?"

"I was a hunter, yes, a hunter of tigers in these very woods."

"You are a hunter again, a hunter of men. You will help me creep up on the invaders who shamed us all."

"Captain. Sir." The NCO was nervous. He did not want to say anything that would cause the pistol to be yanked from its holster again. "I would do all you ask. But I must advise you that I was not a good tracker. I simply used bait and lured the tigers to me. I will do the best I can in following these men, but—"

Tat Thant raised his wounded hand like a traffic cop, and the NCO flinched. "Then do your best."

Tat Thant followed his NCO up the slope at the quickest pace he could manage. At first, it was not much. The bandages, tight as they were, chafed his wounds. At first, he walked with his arms stiff, barely able to bend his knees. He realized he must look like a wooden doll, a puppet poorly handled. From behind him he thought he heard the sound of a giggle. That did not bother him. The man who had tried to kill him with the automatic rifle, that bothered him, yes. The private who had refused, however innocently, to go after the terrorists, that bothered him.

But a man able to snicker at him after he had already killed two others, that was either brave or foolhardy. Tat Thant did not want to take the spirit out of his men. He wanted brave and foolhardy soldiers behind him, not cowering fools.

In only twenty minutes, his muscles had limbered up. The

medications on his wounds had eased his pain. He felt a bit light-headed but capable of coherent thinking.

NIGHT RUNNER HAD checked their tiny camp's perimeter, both at the edge of the thicket and for fifty meters out, after advising the rest of the team that he would be making a circuit. He found no evidence of trails within either perimeter. That helped him relax when he got back inside the thicket and lay down to sleep.

Less than an hour later, he awakened with a jerk.

The movement caught Swayne's attention. The captain looked at him across a distance of only fifteen feet and asked a question by raising his eyebrows. Night Runner put a finger to his lips. He did not want to talk about it over the air.

Out of habit, Night Runner checked in all directions, using each of his senses, one by one and then in combination, before moving out of his position. As the temperature rose, the jungle had grown quiet, except for the gathering of the Montagnard and the Marine colonel in the ravine. Night Runner was glad that their conversation would be directed upward by the walls of the cleft in the earth. How could two people find so much to talk about from a war of nearly thirty years ago? Since he had been in the Force Recon team, he had never heard Swayne give a debriefing to his superiors a fraction that long.

When he was satisfied that nothing had changed in the sights, sounds, smells, tastes, and feel of the jungle, he crept to Swayne's position and knelt by his captain. They both shut off their mikes.

"What's up?" Swayne asked. "The way you came out of your sleep, I thought you heard something."

"Negative. Something has been bothering me ever since we torched that missile—no, before we torched it."

Swayne nodded. Squinting, he nibbled at his lower lip. "The reaction force? Is that it?"

"Exactly. How did they know to commit both security

forces from the head and the tail of the convoy at once?"

"An alarm, you think? The refuelers?"

"That's what I've been thinking. Maybe when I disconnected the static ground line from the truck. Maybe somebody was supposed to make a radio call once the refueling started. Maybe somebody in the refueling shack saw something suspicious. Maybe we tripped an alarm wire when we came out of the forest."

Swayne kept his silence. Some of those very ideas had crossed his mind. Nothing that he could confirm. "Does it matter?"

Night Runner kept his front teeth together. "I thought not. That's why I didn't say anything. If somebody had set off an alarm, it didn't matter because we had destroyed the missile, the trucks, the works."

"And?"

"Now I'm not so sure. I've played this thing through my mind a dozen times. So many times I can't be sure which images in my head actually happened and which are speculations."

"Right." Swayne understood that. Nobody could over-analyze a situation better than he could. Sometimes there was no way to reconcile—"Wait. We could check out the instant replay."

Swayne dug into his pack and produced the night vision binoculars. After a few seconds of trying to read the tiny print on the buttons, he gave up. He closed his eyes and began working the control panels with his fingertips. He knew his way around the binoculars better in the dark than by day. Finally he had it. He looked into the binoculars and rewound the digital images back to a point before all hell broke loose.

"Here it is." He kept the pictures running and described the action in a low voice. "The guard is walking along the truck cab. The Montagnard comes out of nowhere and stands up, his back to the missile carrier. The soldier doesn't see a thing. He touches the Montagnard and jumps away. He's fumbling with his rifle. The Montagnard coldcocks him and goes for the cab of the truck. I can't see what is going on where you were. The Montagnard opens the door of the truck and pulls something from his ammo belt. His knife, I think. The security force reacts at both ends of the road. How? Whoa—"

"What?"

Swayne looked up from the binoculars, closed his eyes, and began working the buttons on the control panel. "I'll rewind it. You see for yourself. See if you come to the same conclusion as me." Swayne began to run the replay forward and handed the binoculars over.

Night Runner watched the pictures run forward, listening to the audio that would identify the moment when the re-action force had been alerted. "I missed it. Rewind a few frames and let me see again."

Swayne took the controls for a moment, then handed the binoculars back.

"I got it." Night Runner looked up from the binoculars and into Swayne's eyes. Both of them began to nod. Both had gone against their natural tendencies to follow the main action on the tiny video screen. Both had looked away from the suspenseful moment when the Montagnard produced his stiletto, which he used to kill the Vietnamese soldier in the cabin of the truck. It was the briefest of moments, barely two seconds worth of video.

The Vietnamese sentry lay on his back, clutching his throat. Then, in desperation, he reached for his belt buckle. The first time Swayne had seen it, he thought he might be pulling a radio or a pistol. But he did not. He worked with the buckle and then lost consciousness, his hands falling to his sides. Within five seconds, a radio signal must have gone out. Both security forces dashed to their trucks and sped toward the refueling site.

"Our prisoner," said Swayne. "He must be wearing a transmitter." They looked at each other, both their jaws set, both their minds focused on the same question. "In his belt."

Night Runner asked it aloud. "You think it's directional?"

"No way to know just yet, but even if it's not a true personal locator beacon, a direction-finding receiver could pinpoint it."

"If it's still transmitting."

"We'd better find out if it is. You take over security for a minute, I'll go get him."

As Swayne gathered himself to stand up, Night Runner patted the air in front of his own chest. "Wait. Sir. Let's think about that for a second. He's down in that little gully. If it is transmitting, the signal is being shielded."

"Which still means that this is the last spot where a clear signal might have been sent out. Before the colonel and the Montagnard took him down there."

Swayne looked at his watch. "Almost two hours," he said.

They both knew what that meant. They had directed dozens of attacks on enemy forces that had been spotted and targeted. By now half the Vietnamese army could have been mobilized. Swayne knew that their Air Force still had American helicopters left over from Vietnam, resupplied by spare parts from China, which had created an entire industry of reverse engineering American technology—even outdated technology.

Right now, airmobile troops could be on the way. Worse, fighter jets. Worst of all, bombers.

Swayne, who had been feeling sluggish from the heat after last night's freezing operation, came wide awake. Both he and Night Runner turned on their radio sets at once. Both understood the urgency, as Swayne spoke calmly so as not to induce panic: "Team this is Spartan One. Saddle up. We march in one minute."

Night Runner clasped his fist over his microphone as if he were catching a mosquito. "Do you have a plan?"

Swayne covered his own boom mike and gave it to him,

making it up as he went along. When he had finished, he raised his eyebrows.

Night Runner's mouth formed the letter *U* upside down: *Not bad.* "Any idea how you're going to handle—"

"What the hell is going on?" Zavello growled as he joined them.

Swayne shot a quick glance at Night Runner, telling him to get moving with a shifting of his eyes. Then he took a deep breath to deal with Zavello.

Zavello spoke first. "I can see something's up. Just give me the short version. We can trade details later."

Swayne exhaled, his sigh an expression of thanks. "The prisoner might have a transmitter on him." Swayne caught a movement coming out of the ravine. Night Runner held up the belt and nodded. "That confirms it. The prisoner did have a transmitter on him. Which means a reaction force might be on the way."

Zavello was quick on the uptake. "Or the whole Communist Air Force." He looked at the sky. "What's your plan, Captain?"

Swayne assembled the group, leaving Friel and Greiner to provide security along their back trail. Night Runner, carrying the belt with its extra thick buckle and foot-long strand of wire that was clearly the antenna, worn inside the sentry's trousers, led the rest of the group en masse out of the thicket toward the clearing. Swayne brought up the rear. They had gone only twenty meters when Night Runner turned around.

"About-face, everybody," he announced. "Stay roughly on the same path back into the foliage."

Once they were back inside the thicket, Swayne directed Friel and Greiner to walk out through the grass along the path.

"Turn around, then come back?" asked Friel.

"You got it, Henry. Now go."

In the clearing, Night Runner used one of his old tricks, stomping the grass at three spots to mimic a helicopter LZ:

two points at which the front tires would press down the grass, and one where the tail wheel would rest. Before he joined up with Greiner and Friel on the way back to the thicket, he dropped off the belt at the end of the track through the grass. At one point along the trail, he turned to plant a boot print in an anthill. The grass, bent over in the right direction, pointed to the takeoff spot. After he returned to cover, he looked back out toward the clearing. If the Vietnamese did not have an expert tracker, Swayne's plan would work.

Anybody with a direction-finding receiver would follow it to the spot where Night Runner had dropped the belt. Troops would converge on the spot. The force would recognize the trail ending meant that a helicopter had lifted them out.

Now came the tricky part. He would have to clean up any evidence of their true departure from the thicket. Assuming that an enemy aircraft force might already be on the way toward the spot, they did not have much time.

Swayne led his troops on a compass heading that would take them to the foothills area, a spot where woodcutters had cleared enough of the forest to allow a helicopter to extract them. Swayne remembered the spot from his photo reconnaissance in the premission briefing. Using his handheld computer, he called up photos to confirm and briefed Zavello about their rally point.

Zavello nodded in appreciation. "Looks good for what I have in mind," he said.

Swayne stared a moment, waiting to hear what that might be.

"Details later."

"Captain Swayne?" the Montagnard said, holding out a hand.

Swayne remembered. He owed the man a pouch of gold, his payment packed away deep in his pack.

Zavello took the flat man's hand. "Later, Monty, he'll pay you later. I'm not finished catching up on the old times."

The Montagnard smiled on one side of his face and dropped his hand.

"As soon as we get to our next stopping point," Swayne reassured him.

Swayne led out, putting the Montagnard, the prisoner, Greiner, Zavello, then Friel in file behind him. As they moved out of the thicket, Night Runner called after them, "Try to walk in the same footsteps."

He took the broom and plastic fan that he had used on previous missions from his backpack. He brushed away every trace of a boot print that pointed the way his troops had taken. Then he fanned the dust until the minilandscape looked natural. Once he had cleared the thicket, the task was slightly tougher. Whereas he had wanted a track to show in the grass before, now that became problematic. Swayne had done his best to keep to the undergrowth, but each time Night Runner found grass, it took him a long time to straighten up the stalks and make it look natural from the ground. In fact, it would not look natural from the air for another month or two when fresh grass had grown up to hide the evidence of broken stalks.

Night Runner had been in this situation before, in Iraq, when he had underestimated his enemy, and the Bedouin tracker had nearly run them to ground. He would not make that mistake again. He made a quick call to Swayne, telling his captain that he would remain behind to assess the enemy situation.

"Steer clear of the LZ, in case they decide to shoot long-range artillery or hit it with air strikes," Swayne said.

"Wilco." Night Runner downloaded new map sets for the area, from radar satellite imagery. He drew a straight line from the spot where they had destroyed the missile to the fake LZ, where he had dropped the transmitter. A quick study of the terrain told him the most likely routes any re-action force would have to take. Then he simply plotted a course that would help him intercept his enemy, if one came.

Night Runner was glad to be alone in the jungle. Now that he did not have to worry about the rest of the team and the distractions of having a prisoner, a guide, and of all things, a senior staff officer in the field keeping his one good eye on things, Night Runner could focus. He had seen enough of Monty to realize just how far he had to go to sharpen his own tracking skills in the tropical forest. Not since the Bedouin had he felt so upset by the prowess of another warrior with skills better than his own. He was glad that the Montagnard warrior was an ally. On the other hand, he was embarrassed. Enemy or no, the man was superior to him in the skills in which he took the most personal pride. Night Runner already knew that he would be spending his next vacation in the Everglades or some other swamp. He had to bring himself up to the level of the Montagnard in a jungle setting. If possible, he had to exceed him. For he knew that, if a man existed as an ally with such skills, surely there must be an enemy equally capable. If he should ever have to face a man like that, Night Runner needed to prepare.

He would not waste a second more of his life worrying about his lack of skill. He would sharpen up now.

As he moved through the forest, he imagined himself a cat. He had studied the animal on the Discovery Channel. He had watched cats in the Wild North American forests, including the cougar, the bobcat, and the rare lynx. When those animals began their stalk, they could vanish before your eyes. They could move without disturbing the dust— or so it seemed to all but a tracker like himself.

This was how he crept through the forest. Each time a dry leaf crackled beneath his boots, he rated it a blunder. Each time a twig scraped against the fabric of his clothing, he cringed at the flub.

He stopped once to remove his jacket and trousers. He stuffed them into his pack. Now when a twig touched him, his skin gave him warning. He could flinch or recoil, avoiding all noise.

He stopped a second time to remove his boots and socks. He left his pack and his boots. He rested the barrel of his Brat ultralight machine gun across the pile of gear. That, too, would stay behind. He was a better warrior without it.

He kept his radio, packing it into the waistband of his camo underwear briefs. If he should have to make contact with Swayne, or in the more likely case that Swayne wanted to contact him, he would have to have his tactical ears and mouth. He crept through the undergrowth, moving a step at a time, stopping, listening, stepping, stopping. His feet were not as tough as the Montagnard's. But they were not as soft as those of the white men on his team, either. Even so, he had a greater sensitivity for the earth now, perhaps greater than even the Montagnard. That he suffered the occasional prick of a thorn or sting of an ant was just another lesson in his craft.

It surprised him how much quieter he could move without clothing. Still, he was not as silent as the Montagnard. And he lacked the dark tan of Monty—beneath his clothing, he'd begun to whiten. He need to darken himself in the sun, to wear his skin as camouflage. He compensated by moving like the ferret, darting from tree to tree to bush to boulder.

At each stop, brief as it was, he tallied each of his senses. Listening. Seeing. Smelling. Tasting. Touching. Until at last his nose and mouth told him of a human presence before he could see or hear it.

The air smelled of medicine mingled with sweat and the scent of cooked flesh. He crouched low, putting his only weapon before his eyes as he looked beneath the undergrowth. That weapon was the scimitar he'd taken from the Bedouin those many missions ago.

Finally, he saw the man he was looking for. Not twenty meters away, visible walking at an odd gait through the trees. He counted four, no, five men in all. That worried him.

Night Runner looked all around him, especially to his rear. Perhaps a larger enemy force was moving forward in squad-level units or smaller. Perhaps they were canvassing the whole area, looking for sign of the men who had attacked their missiles.

When he could detect no sign of anybody else, he concentrated on the five, a ragged bunch. One of them looked like a walking wound, mostly bandaged, with his exposed skin the color and texture of a chocolate chip cookie. Night Runner realized that the man's skin was badly burned and oozing through his clothing. The group took a short break, with two of the healthy soldiers offering canteens of water to the wounded man. Obviously an officer. He drained both canteens. Then he turned to vomit into the trees.

His men surrounded him, supporting him. He shook himself free. He pointed again, and spoke in guttural barks. The group moved out, following a tentative tracker. Night Runner saw they were headed toward the landing zone, crashing through the foliage.

He couldn't believe that such a small group would be the only force dispatched against the Force Recon team. The group were not special operations types. From the wounds and lack of stealth in the forest, these were just members of the force guarding the missile, and not a well-disciplined unit, at that.

Carefully, slowly, he checked all around him. Still nothing. He crept back toward where he had left his clothing and pack. He would need the light machine gun if there were more men, and they surprised him. He did not expect that, but he was not so arrogant as to dismiss the possibility.

He decided to remain barefoot. The pack would make some noise in the forest, but he could not afford to leave it behind.

He dug out his GPS receiver. As he tuned in the frequency of his own PERLOBE, he got an idea. He began dialing through the PERLOBE's frequency range, stopping at every detent. He smiled at the sudden flickering on the LED screen. The receiver had picked up a PERLOBE with a frequency not assigned to one of the team. The directional arrow pointed to where he'd left the Vietnamese sentry's belt. Suspicion confirmed. The device was more than an alarm; it was a beacon. Very likely the French, who had stolen and sold the technology, had let it fall into the hands of the Vietnamese. That meant that every Communist country in the world had it as well. Once it had circulated to the communist countries, it was a small leap to reach the hands of terrorist organizations like al Qaida and regimes like that of Saddam Hussein.

He put a finger to the On-Off button of the receiver, but a second inspiration struck him, so he did not turn it off. Instead, he kept whirling the dial a stop at a time. A second receiver, also of an unknown frequency, showed up on the screen. The arrow pointed in the same direction. He checked the azimuth of both beacons. No, not exactly the same. Perhaps half a degree apart in direction. It could only mean one thing. Somehow, there were two beacons on roughly the same line to the LZ. Perhaps two beacons lay in the LZ right now. *How could that be?*

He decided he needed to find out. Securing his gear as tightly as he could, he tried to make his pack as narrow as possible, so it would have less bulk to scrape against the foliage.

Once he was satisfied, he crossed the trail behind the five Vietnamese soldiers. He moved into the forest, taking barely two steps at a time. The last thing he wanted was to run into another five-man unit following up the first.

TAT THANT WISHED he had some way to know how close they were getting to his enemies.

He felt his strength draining in the ooze seeping through his bandages. Even if they were to find their enemy, he might not have energy enough to fight them. The forest had begun to shimmer in front of him, like a mirage over the sea near his home at Da Nang. The trees had become vertical snakes, dancing in place.

He could not slake his thirst. The more he drank, the more he wanted, but even a little more was too much. His stomach rejected it. He had tried the water with salt pills and without. Nothing made a difference anymore. His men, who had been surly at first, had taken pity on him. That did not help. It only made him angry. He wanted to kill the terrorists, and it did not seem as if he would live long enough to do it.

He felt that way up until the moment one of his men grabbed his arm. The pain of it forced him to drop to his knees. He had to check the shoulder socket to see that the arm had not been torn off his body.

Eventually the pain passed, and he realized that he was surrounded by his men. They were kneeling, whispering to him.

Both the pain and his lack of ears made it difficult for him to hear. Finally he understood what his noncom had been trying to tell him. He could read the man's urgent lips.

"Somebody has been here."

Tat Thant smiled. He looked around himself. They were in a cool place, a thicket as dark as the inside of a hut. Once his eyes adjusted, he could see boot tracks on the ground. Several men. A set of bare feet. The noncom pointed toward a doorway in the foliage leading out of the thicket toward the open.

Tat Thant moved into the light. There, ahead of him, he could see a dark, wide trail in the chest-high grass.

The noncom spoke to him again.

"What?" he said.

He read the lips again: *Helicopter landing area.*

"No," he sighed in desperation. "It cannot be. I'll go see."

"Sir, let me go."

Tat Thant stood up and took one step. His men grabbed for him but missed. He vanished. He had stepped out, not onto a dark path but into a deep ravine. Falling felt like flying. It seemed a long time before he hit the ground. One sharp moment of pain, and then it was over. In the instant before he lost consciousness, tat Thant felt a moment of regret that he would not be able to kill the invaders. Then as his pain faded with his consciousness, he was simply glad to be going wherever his new wings would take him.

As he slept, he became aware of the monsoon rains hitting the tin roof of his father's farmhouse near the Da Nang coast, making a noise as loud and regular as gunfire.

NIGHT RUNNER HIT the ground at the first sound of the ambush. He did not hear the report of the rifles at first, just the crack of bullets whacking the trees nearby, some of them singing the angry song of the ricochet. He pushed the muzzle of his Brat out ahead of him but held his fire. Something was not right. All the gunfire was being shot far too high over his head to be aimed at him. He rolled over onto his back and looked into the trees. Except for an occasional ricochet that bent a slug downward toward him, all the bullets sang by overhead, twenty to thirty feet or higher in the foliage.

So, he reasoned, the ambush was not for him but for somebody else. He had simply gotten himself directly beyond the line of fire of the intended target. From all the shooting going on, the *sisss-crack-boom* explosions of rocket-propelled grenades, he knew most of the firing came from a force much larger than the five men ahead of him.

He began inching backward, not wanting to be in position to be caught up in a sweep of the kill zone that would follow this battle.

As far as he knew, he did not even hear any return fire. Likely, the five men had died in the first strike.

That explained the frequency of the second beacon. The ambush force must have had a beacon of its own, transmitting to their own headquarters. Ironic. Force Recon Marines had stopped using PERLOBEs after the technology had been stolen, fearful of getting struck by artillery aimed at their transmitters. Now that the Americans had made their transmitters immune to such detection, the people who had stolen and benefited from the beacons would suffer from it; they could be located and targeted. He made a mental note for the after-action brief.

Soon after he had gotten well clear, the shooting died down. He made a wide circuit, retracing his tracks, moving even farther out than before.

Only once, as he was crossing a ridgeline, could he look back to get an idea of what had happened.

Through his binoculars he saw a large force, perhaps as much as a battalion, milling around in the landing zone. From what he could see, the force had surrounded the clearing. Perhaps they were moving in on the thicket, the closest cover to the Vietnamese sentry's beacon when the five men walked out into the open. That would account for the furious attack.

Night Runner's concern for the five Vietnamese was no concern at all. All he worried about was what would happen next. He decided to hustle through the jungle to intercept the Spartans' trail. He would set up security so he could watch their six, so he would know if anybody in the battalion found the Force Recon team's tracks leading away from the thicket. He would act the Blackfeet warrior of old, using the tricks of the animals of Montana.

He would become the antelope on the plains when menaced by a pack of coyotes. Coyotes would never be fast enough to run down an antelope. But they might pull a sneak and catch a herd unawares, perhaps spread out, and snatch a fawn. That's why one of the lead does or herd buck would move toward the coyotes, keeping track of them at all times. If they did follow the team, he would ease away as the PAVN approached, keeping his distance, yet keeping contact. He would become an antelope in the forest, keeping track of the Vietnamese coyotes, letting Swayne and the others know if they would be in danger from this battalion.

After two hours of watching, the Vietnamese had not come. Night Runner was satisfied that the enemy had not found the team's tracks, had bought into the helicopter ruse, and would not be following the team. Only then did he catch up with the Spartans at their new rally point.

THE CENTRAL HIGHLANDS, VIETNAM
1654 HOURS LOCAL

SWAYNE PULLED THE plug on his anxiety the moment Night Runner spoke up in his earpiece to say that he had joined up.

"What's your position?" Swayne asked.

"Just north of your perimeter."

"Roger, I'll alert the others that you're coming in."

Night Runner made a quick check of his equipment as he dressed in his regular Force Recon gear. The rest of the team had seen him in primitive warrior dress before, but he did not want to reveal anything about the tactic to Zavello, the Montagnard, or even the prisoner. Zavello, grown rusty and soft from desk duty, would not get it. Being a ranking officer put him in the position of having to object to anything not done exactly by the book, and a near-naked fighting Marine could be found nowhere in that book. Not that Zavello was a bad person. Only that long periods away from the field tended to put a straitjacket around an officer's mind. What's more, Runner did not want their prisoner to see him in his true tactical mode. The less Zavello and the sentry knew, the better.

Finally, as a point of pride, Night Runner did not want the Montagnard to know that he had skinned off his white man's clothing to be more like this original native of Vietnam. No sense in boosting the Montagnard's ego by revealing that Night Runner would imitate him.

Usually he did not announce himself before entering a Force Recon perimeter. But the Montagnard would spot him. And, if by accident the raw Marine colonel saw him, he did not want to be shot.

Once inside the perimeter, Night Runner sized up the situation. He could not see the Montagnard, so he assumed he had been paid off and sent on his way. The Vietnamese prisoner used his fingers to pick pieces of meal out of a foil packet, while Greiner stood guard over him. Night Runner had to smile. It looked like Thai chicken, one of the meals with rice. A nice gesture on somebody's part, but an awful choice for an Oriental. The chicken tasted as if it had been prepared in ketchup and peanut butter. The rice had the consistency of the snap, crackle, pop cereal left to soak too long in milk. Once he began burping, the man would hate Thailand as much as America.

Friel caught his eye. He gave a wiseass grin and a sloppy, two-finger Cub Scout salute: *welcome to the circus*. Then Friel returned his attention to the jungle on his side of the perimeter.

The captain lifted his chin, and Night Runner joined him at the side of the perimeter opposite Friel. Zavello lay ten feet away, pulling a turn at sentry. Night Runner flipped his gaze in the colonel's direction, asking the question in body language. In answer, Swayne closed his eyes in a triple-length blink and nodded once, slowly. The gesture told Night Runner to give his report over the radio. It made sense for everybody to hear at once, including Zavello and intelligence analysts in the Operational Mission Control Center on the other side of the earth, real-time plus three seconds away.

So Night Runner gave his news to anybody in the Force Recon community in the world who had a receiver and the right frequency that included a scrambler. In his brief style he told how the regular battalion ambushed the five ragged soldiers. The battle was marked by slow, tentative tactics on the part of the regulars. They would fire in mad-minute style, cutting loose with everything they had, supported by mortars and rockets, wasting tons of ammunition. The fire had cut tops out of several trees in the thicket, telling Night Runner that many of the soldiers were shooting blind at their mates hunkered down inside the thicket. After several five-minute stretches like this, the regulars tried to advance. One rifle shot from within the thicket set off another frenzy of fire.

Eventually, one company of regulars maneuvered to the flank of the minisquad. There only problem was that they maneuvered too far and came at the small force from behind. They shot through the thicket into their own on the other side. Two more periods of unrestrained shooting followed.

Finally, the shooting had died down.

"Probably because the entire battalion had shot up its basic load of ammunition," Night Runner said. "I couldn't see everything, but two, maybe three of the guys in the squad survived, even after all that. At least a dozen of the battalion were carried out on litters, maybe half of those dead, probably shot in the back."

That was the entertaining part of his report. Runner gave the important part in his last sentence: "After the battalion tramped through the area, they could not have found any sign of us with a forensics team; they gathered up their dead and dying and took off back toward the road."

Swayne asked, "They didn't leave any scouts? Rear guard?"

"None. I spent another hour checking before heading back here."

Zavello chimed in. "Funny thing. In the early part of the Vietnam war, green American units fought like that. For a long time, the South Vietnamese did the same thing—shooting out of their foxholes straight up into the air, clip after clip of ammunition. Just making noise. The sign of troops without discipline. Funny."

Nobody said anything because it wasn't really all that funny. Ironic though, that the army that had been at one time the most combat-hardened of any in the world had lost its edge.

Zavello spoke after a minute's silence. "I suppose you're all wondering why I called you together." Nobody reacted to the question. Zavello shrugged. "It's an old joke from Vietnam. It used to break us up every time we heard it."

Swayne and Night Runner gave him a weak smile.

"You had to be there, I guess."

Swayne understood. During combat, emotions were strained to the breaking point. Potts, their original gunny, killed in Iraq, used to make remarks that broke up the group. A Marine at the point of exhaustion could find the dumbest remark hilarious; a look could create a laughing jag a half-hour long. It all depended on the timing, the fatigue factor, and the jokester. Zavello would never cut it as a combat comic. People were too used to dodging his threats. They might laugh behind his back, but few had the nerve even to risk smiling to his face. Especially this audience. Swayne's Force Recon team had had Zavello in their earpiece every time they went out in the past three years. Three years' worth of ass-chewings, and now a joke? Not a chance.

Zavello blinked twice with his one eye. "I have a new mission for Team 2400.

EVENT SCENARIO 23

KHE SANH PROVINCE, VIETNAM
11APR02—1741 HOURS LOCAL

ZAVELLO WENT RIGHT to the point. "Augmented by me,
Force Recon team 2400 is to conduct reconnaissance on a
suspected detention camp for MIAs and POWs surviving
from the Vietnam War preparatory to a rescue raid by American Special Operations forces."

As he said it, he looked into Swayne's eyes.

Swayne took his turn to blink. First because Zavello's evil
eye and craggy face had a strange quality to it, a kind of
hateful compassion. Second, and most striking, because his
own father had gone missing in action in Vietnam. Although
the Pentagon had declared him dead decades ago, nobody
had ever produced remains.

Zavello's briefing didn't last long nor was it laden with
details. A defector from Communist Vietnam had reported
the presence of MIAs and POWs. The Defense Department
took all such reports seriously—not necessarily because they
believed them but because they were much more interested

in damage control. Veterans' groups, wives, and families of MIAs and POWs never dismissed a report coming out of Southeast Asia; rather, they clung to it. Veterans' groups never lost interest in the topic, a source of their patriotic passion. No politician dared show a lack of concern. Besides, plenty of soldiers in uniform, even if they had no direct tie to the Vietnam War, could never accept that America would abandon its soldiers; it was too personal, too frightening. It did not make good sense for any of the services to suggest that people in uniform did not matter. Only when enough time had passed for anybody from a previous war to be dead, could a myth like surviving MIAs and POWs be dismissed.

Unlike many of the previous unfounded reports out of Vietnam, many of them hoaxes, Zavello said, this one had specifics: "People spotted were Caucasian, at least two dozen, possibly as many as forty. They were the right ages— fifties and sixties. They were slave laborers with occupations ranging from farmers to simple craftsmen to skilled trades-men." He bit his lower lip. "Best part is, we got a specific location. Grid coordinates. Allegedly from a guard in the labor camp. An eye witness. The guy faked his death in Ho Chi Minh City so he could defect."

Swayne barely heard Zavello telling how he had picked up the report at the Operational Mission Control Center when an information-only summary of two reports crossed his desk just days ago. How he had a need-to-know coordination in-terest because of the Force Recon team operating against the missile carrier that Night Runner had destroyed. How Zav-ello had ordered himself into the field because Swayne's team had orders for their strike mission within eight hours' march of the suspected labor camp.

Swayne sat stunned after Zavello had finished his briefing. The colonel asked for questions. Swayne had one but lacked the courage to ask it. He caught Zavello's gaze boring into him, eye-to-eyes.

"Out with it," Zavello said with a snarl.

Swayne shrugged and twitched his head.

"I said, out with it."

"Sir. Why—?" He raised the palms of both hands.

"Why did I come out here? Why not just call it in and put you boys on it?"

"Yes, sir." Swayne doubted it was a lack of confidence in the team. Still. A simple radio call. All the team needed to know were coordinates and mission. The Spartans could pull the recon: a cursory look would take no more than a few hours. A detailed report with enough information for a co-ordinated raid might take only a couple days. It did not make sense to augment the team. Even a second Force Recon team, although it might save time in gathering information, would increase the chances of being detected on the insertion or during the recon. Putting a fifty-year-old, one-eyed colonel with no recent combat or even field experience on the ground—

"You don't think an over-the-hill bastard with one eye can contribute?" It was not so much a question as a dare for Swayne to speak the very thought on his mind.

No way, he thought. *No way in—*

Zavello's stiff posture wilted. "Shut off the microphones," he said. He leaned close to Swayne. "You might be right, Captain. There's no good operational reason for me to be here. Hell, you *are* right. I heard the name, Monty. I thought I would come out here to see if it was the same guy who worked with me when I was a guide and needed somebody to hold my hand on long-range reconnaissance operations. It was. So court-martial me."

Swayne looked away, embarrassed for the colonel. The man had just confessed to having a heart, all evidence to the contrary. This trip was, to him, perhaps a journey to the elephant's graveyard to die. Maybe he'd already put in papers to retire. Maybe he just needed one last fling with an elevated adrenaline level.

Zavello laughed a wicked laugh. "Now I'm here, in the

middle of the shit, I'm big enough to admit it was a mistake. All my piss and vinegar is in my head. The body doesn't cut it anymore. A little lack of sleep out here isn't the same as pulling a sixteen-hour shift at the OMCC." He picked up a pebble and tossed it at a tree trunk. "That little two-bit march we took today busted my ass. It's not the same as an hour on the stair-stepper and a five-mile jog after work."

A weak, wicked smile betrayed a pain much sharper than aged legs and arthritic knees. "Now you're stuck with me. I'm about as useless as that Vietnamese kid. I can pull my share of grunt details. I'll pull guard detail on the prisoner and let you run the show. I'll keep my nose out of it."

Swayne could not prevent a half-smile from pulling at the left side of his face.

"Okay, so I won't be able to stop myself from sticking my nose into it. I give you permission to ignore me."

Swayne let the other side of his face complete the smile.

"My word as a Marine, Swayne."

Swayne went sober. A Marine had given his word. No matter that he was a colonel, his superior in rank as well as age. It would have meant as much coming from any Marine. No smiling matter.

"Roger, sir."

Zavello lifted one corner of his upper lip. "Until we get back to the world. Then you're going to debrief me, same as always. You screw up out here, and I'm going to be on your ass. This time you're not going to be able to hide things from me by turning off your microphone."

At that moment Swayne understood Zavello better than at any time before. The man simply acted tough because that's what everybody expected him to be. But Swayne saw in the eye a glimpse of a father figure. Zavello knew Swayne had lost his father out here, that the man had been presumed dead.

Zavello spoke softly. "I talked to Monty about the camp.

He confirms it. I can tell you this: the Joint Chiefs are serious about a rescue operation. If we find men in there, we'll get them out. You can take that to the bank."

SWAYNE TOOK ZAVELLO up on his offer to guard the prisoner, giving Greiner time to rest. Then he took Night Runner and Friel off the perimeter as well. He needed a break, too, but he would use the remaining hours of daylight to download fresh maps and the latest intelligence updates from the OMCC. He gave the team a warning order, an official heads-up to be ready to march at twilight with a mission to recon the suspected camp. Later he would give everybody instructions in greater detail, in the form of a five-paragraph field order.

Even with multiple tasks, Swayne finished his work in an hour. He had plenty of time to rest, but not the frame of mind. For a change, it wasn't planning the mission that distracted him, his usual practice of searching a situation from end to end, back to front, side to side, looking for every possible angle at which something could go wrong, preparing alternatives for the lot. No, for the first time in a long time, he was overcome by memories, feelings, and regrets. These things he could usually keep out of his head until he returned to the States. Not this time. This time it was personal. This time it had to do with his father. He could trust his men to carry out their orders. He could trust himself to deal with contingencies as they came up. He could war-game every situation but one. He had no clue about how to behave when it came time to rescue American prisoners, one of whom might be his own father. How were a father and a son supposed to behave after all that time when one of them was presumed dead?

TAT THANT KNEW that he had awakened at a hospital before he ever opened his eyes. The antiseptic smell told him all he needed to know. The only question was, how had he survived? He remembered the shooting, he remembered falling, and he remembered a painful journey, people carrying him as he fell in and out of consciousness. He also remembered calling out, asking someone to kill him, to somehow make the pain go away. He hoped that part had been a dream. He wouldn't want to wake up and discover that he had behaved badly.

Then again, the more awake he felt, the more he felt the flames burning through his head and the back of this entire body. It took all his will to keep from crying out, from begging for death to come.

"He's conscious," a voice said. "See here. See how his pulse rate has increased."

Tat Thant felt a shriek growing in his chest. Why had they allowed him to awaken at all? He wanted to scream, to cry, to curse at these idiots. He would have, except for the next voice he heard.

"Can I talk to him?"

"Father?" The word escaped tat Thant's lips as a hiss.

"Yes, my son."

"I'm sorry, Father." All at once tat Thant forgot about the nerve ends on fire over more than half his body. A greater pain stabbed him at his core. The pain of shaming his country and his family. The pain of having his father stand here and share in the disgrace. If only he had not fallen into the gully when the firefight broke out. He would have charged his enemy. He would have tried to redeem himself by killing some of them before being killed himself.

"My son, something dreadful has happened."

"I know," tat Thant whimpered. "I allowed an army of terrorists to destroy one of our strategic missiles. Then I allowed the enemy to ambush me and my small unit. I'm afraid they have gotten away. I am ashamed to be the only one who survived."

"Oh, no, that's not what happened."

Tat Thant opened his eyes. He found himself lying on his

belly, his face supported by rolls of bandages. The mere attempt to lift his head and turn it caused a blowtorch to be ignited at the back in his neck. Against his will, he cried out.

"Lie still," his father said, his voice soothing. "Give him something for his pain," he ordered.

Tat Thant felt the air stirring as somebody moved around his bed. He realized he was lying naked, his burns exposed to the air. Even the slightest draft seemed as wicked as a lash of bamboo strips. In a few seconds, he grew drowsy and realized somebody must have dripped narcotics into one of the tubes in the backs of his hands. His lips tingled. He could still feel the pain in his back. But the drug, whatever it was, allowed him to step away from it.

"What happened?" he murmured.

His father told him about the ambush by the PAVN battalion. Hearing the facts did not allow tat Thant to feel any better. In fact, he felt worse. More than ever he wished that he had died.

And must have said so, for his father spoke up to contradict his very thought.

"No, nobody wishes that for you. Two of your men have survived."

"My noncommissioned officer?"

"Yes, he told us of your bravery. Of going after the enemy although you had been burned so seriously, the effort should have killed you."

This time tat Thant bit his lips so he could be sure to keep his wish for death to himself.

Sometime later—he had lost his sense of time, so he knew not how much later—he thought to ask: "Where am I?"

His father told him a name that he did not recognize.

"Why have I never heard of this place?"

"It's the camp that I command."

"And you never told me about it?"

"It is a place so secret that few people outside the highest levels of government and our People's Army know its name.

It was the closest place with a hospital." He explained that it was a slave labor camp for foreigners who could not be trusted to be turned back to their native countries.

"Father, before I die—"

"Son—"

"I must know. Tell me. Who did this to our country?"

The gentle voice hardened. "The Americans. I am sure of it. You rest. I will make them pay for it."

Tat Thant was glad that his father had ordered him to rest. The few minutes he had been awake were painful and exhausting, despite the relief that drugs had given him. Even so, he would have liked to know how his father, great man that he was, and powerful, how could he make the Americans pay? He was certain that those missiles could not be fired across the great ocean, even to the nearest American state, Hawaii. He wanted to ask what could be done. But he could not force his tingling lips to form the words. He fell asleep, once again dreaming about fire.

NIGHT RUNNER HATED Point-A-to-Point-B marches under the best of circumstances. He learned many missions ago in Iraq that it wasn't necessary for an enemy to track him step-by-step. A broken twig here. Disturbed pebbles there. A partial boot track between. One smart guy with a sixth-grade education and a knack for tracking simply had to mark the signs on a map, lay a straightedge down, and connect the dots. Any fool could extend the lines in both directions and identify the starting point and potential destination, simple as that.

He didn't care that his enemy might have fallen for the fake helicopter extraction. He did not get any comfort from knowing that the infantry battalion had picked up its wounded and left the area without even taking time for a simple sweep. Night Runner didn't care how ill-prepared the enemy was. It didn't matter to him what the enemy thought. It only mattered what he and his unit did.

Now he was doing something less than brilliant. He was cutting a straight line through the undergrowth so he could intercept the new Ho Chi Minh Trail. Once there, they were going to hike south on the trail for a full three miles, the best way to cover ground.

Then they would cut off to the southwest, marching another two miles on a straight line to the forest, hoping to get into a position to hide well before dawn. After resting for a couple hours, they would split into two parties to scout the camp for a full twenty-four hours.

Meanwhile, a battalion of staff officers at PaCom, Pacific Command, had began putting together a Delta Force contingent. The Force Recon team's first report would give planners the intel it needed to tailor the force for the operation. He was glad that he'd met Delta Operators and worked with them in the hunt for Osama bin Laden. Maybe he'd hook up on this outing with some old friends.

Night Runner was to lead his own Force Recon team on its first march segment through the forest, picking the easiest path, using game trails where he could find them, keeping to the gentlest slopes. Vietnam had been a rich source of studies about the use of land mines, trip wires, and booby traps in Force Recon training. The Vietcong had devised ingenious methods of killing soldiers who walked on trails and roads, taking the easiest paths. So Runner had forged an aversion to such routes. .

If it had been only the Marines, even with the one-eyed colonel, he would have taken a more difficult path. Leading a prisoner created problems. The Force Recon training program didn't waste effort telling teams how to secure a prisoner and march him through the forests for eight hours. Usually a plan to snatch an enemy VIP or possible source of intelligence included an immediate capability to extract him. Or better, killing him outright.

• • •

SWAYNE AND ZAVELLO agreed that they would first have to confirm to an absolute certainty the presence of Americans. Sightings alone wouldn't be enough. The generals and politicians would demand pictures. Once they had proof of Americans and numbers on the size of both the inmate population and the security force, Delta Force would launch. The rescue force would take off from Hawaii, finishing their insertion planning in the air. They might stage out of Thailand, or they might drop directly from the air, their pickup helicopters coming from carriers cruising the South China Sea.

Swayne resented having a prisoner along. The enemy soldier's presence made him edgy. Night Runner should not have taken him alive. Greiner should not have to divide his attention between guarding the Vietnamese soldier and keeping watch for a threat outside. Zavello should have—

No, face it, Swayne told himself. This wasn't about the prisoner. The distraction was his father. What if they were to find him alive in the prison camp? How would they know each other, except by name? How long would it take to get acquainted? Could they?

His mind began inventing fantasies of their first meeting, and no amount of reason could erase them.

He tried to reassure himself that all the odds were against a reunion. First, his father, a company commander, had disappeared after an intense battle. The remnants of his company had formed small pockets of resistance against a division of North Vietnamese regulars. In a last desperate attempt to save themselves, his father had called for air strikes on their own positions, perhaps on himself. Many of the missing bodies might have been obliterated by U.S. bombs and napalm. Friendly fire, the ultimate irony.

Second, several prisoners from the battle had been taken to Hanoi and repatriated after the war. None of them knew of his father's survival, although they had praised his bravery in the face of huge enemy numbers.

Third, if the Vietnamese had labor camps at all—still

unproven—why would his father be in this one? The Vietnamese might have any number of them scattered up and down the length of their crooked country.

Finally, the only prisoners that might not have been returned, experts had said for years, were those who were too sick or too clearly mistreated by the Vietnamese. They had been kept in captivity to prevent the world getting evidence of human rights violations. Men in such weakened condition might well be left to die, for they could hardly be productive and would be too costly to keep alive.

So, Swayne decided, there was little hope that his father had survived. Yet he could not suppress the fantasies, could not prevent himself from war-gaming the reunion. Rather than working on problems of the camp recon, Swayne let his mind wrestle with the problem of how to recognize a man that he could not remember from his childhood. For he was a toddler when his father left. All he had were pictures from the family photo album. Then only of a man from thirty years ago. If he had survived, it would have been under the most horrible of conditions. He would not be that hardy young man pictured in the uniform of a football player in the tall, muscular body of a tight end. Nor would he be that combat veteran, with one tour in Vietnam already under his belt, his features chiseled from enduring the jungle and battle, his eyes aged yet determined in the photograph on the living room wall. He would be thin, perhaps spent, living on that willpower in the genetic code of all the Swaynes. Above all, he would be older than his years from a tough life in captivity in the tropics. Old. Crippled. Demented. So near death, Swayne feared, he was better dead.

Dark fell, and the team readied to march. Swayne was glad to be back in action that would take his mind—and his heart—off his father. In no time, he had more than enough new distractions.

Problem one was the blindfold. First Swayne thought it a practical move to take it off. But before they had gone ten feet through the underbrush, the man had been snapped across the eyes by a branch, forcing him to cry out in pain through his gag. So Swayne wrapped his head from just above the nostrils to his forehead in an Ace bandage.

Barely three more steps, and a man fell on his face. His hands tied behind his back meant he landed hard, his head whipping forward.

Greiner bent over his captive. "Sorry, man."

Friel muttered into his open mike, "Look at us—the freaking Apple Dumpling Gang."

Swayne fought back a retort, fully aware that his anger was not so much that Friel had spoken up but that he and been right in his assessment. Don Knotts and Tim Conway could not have pulled this off any worse than the Spartans had done so far. With Zavello watching, besides. A simple damned march. They couldn't pull off a simple walk in the woods at night with the most modern night vision goggles in the world. How could he persuade Zavello that any information he had ever given—or ever would give—over the radio would be reliable? The man was watching them screw up by the numbers. How—?

"Jack?"

"Sir?" Zavello could not have stunned him any more if he had whacked him between the eyes with the butt of a rifle. The man had never called him by his first name. Nor had he ever used that tone. The tone in using one word was nothing less than astonishing. "May I?"

Without waiting for permission, Zavello took the Spartans' junior Marine by the elbow. "Greiner?"

"Sir, Corporal Greiner, sir."

"Son, do you think you can secure this prisoner in a way that we can lead him through the jungle without killing his ass?"

"Sir, yes, sir," Greiner said.

"Without losing him, without blinding him, without breaking his face, without him having enough freedom to choke one of us? Can you do all that, son?"

"Sir, yes, sir."

"Do it." He led Swayne away from the group and snipped his two fingers between their faces. Swayne cut off his mike.

"Mine, too."

Swayne took Zavello's hand and showed him how to work the switch.

Zavello moved in too close, like the Montagnard had done, invading his personal space. "Listen, son, I see what's happening here."

"Sir?"

Zavello gave him the traffic cop sign. "Let me talk, Jack. You have a lot of things going. You got me looking over your shoulder. You got a change in mission. You've got that prisoner. And if that isn't enough, you have the picture of your old man running around inside your head, the thought of him being inside that prison, the idea that you might see him."

Swayne opened his mouth but held his tongue when Zavello put up a forefinger between their noses.

"Look, I see it in your face. I'm not blaming you. It's a lot to handle. I don't know if any Marine could—not even me." Zavello took a deep breath.

Swayne feared that the colonel was going to call off the mission. Too many things had already stacked up behind the dam. If somebody came along and pulled just the right twig from the logjam, everything would bust loose from behind it. He knew the sequence: half a dozen tiny glitches, one leading to the other. By itself, no one glitch could bring down a mission. Together they could spell disaster. They even had a name for it in the officer training schools.

"It's the NITA effect, son."

The Negative Impact Trend Accumulation effect, which Friel had recoined the Nail in the Ass effect. According to Friel, "Damned nail falls out, and the horseshoe comes off.

Horseshoe falls off, and the damned horse falls down and breaks the rider's ass. Rider don't deliver his freaking message, the general loses the freaking war. All because of that goddamned nail in the ass."

Nobody ever expected a mission to go perfectly. Nobody would cancel an operation just because one or even several slipups occurred. If perfection had been the measure of battle preparation for humankind, no war would ever have been fought. Some of the greatest disasters had happened because of a succession of related, relatively minor errors and coincidences. This one had all the earmarks of a classic NITA situation. The Force Recon team was operating with the distractions of the prisoner and the visitor. Its leader, Swayne knew, was not in his usual frame of mind, the state where he could foresee problems and prevent them, the ability to swiftly react to unforeseen problems, that capacity to adapt that had made him one of the best small-unit commanders under fire. With his personal demons in play, Swayne knew he was merely mortal now.

"Sir, don't cancel the mission."

"I won't."

Something in his tone of voice told Swayne not to be reassured. "Colonel, you're not thinking of bringing in another Force Recon team?"

"Jack, I'm not going to make the final decision about this operation. You are."

Swayne opened his mouth, then shut it. Zavello had just defined leadership to him. Now it was up to Swayne to exercise it.

His first reaction was simply to blurt, *Let's do it.* That wasn't leadership. *"Damn the torpedoes"* was a nifty saying. Hollywood loved it, which was reason enough not to trust it. In this situation, there were no torpedoes. Just the land mines in his own head.

"I'll leave you alone," Zavello said. "See if I can be some

help to that kid, Greiner. I doubt it. He's a good one. He's a keeper, Jack."

Swayne nodded. Zavello was telling him more than he was saying. Of course Greiner was a good Marine. Night Runner and Swayne would never have taken him out on a second mission if he had failed to show promise on his first. But Zavello was saying, *Don't risk losing a good kid because of your pride, because of your fantasy about your father, because your boss made the mistake of leaving his office to come to a place where he didn't belong.* Swayne understood.

Zavello wasn't merely opening the door so Swayne could correct his potential problems. He was also allowing the captain to place some of the blame on the colonel's shoulders. Zavello knew that he had jinxed the situation. If Swayne called it off, he would be letting the colonel off the hook as well.

Swayne gave Zavello his due. He had always respected the man for his rank, his position, his experience. But he had also thought of him as any other superior officer. Somebody back at headquarters. A glorified staff officer, rather than a field commander. Soldiers in the field had always felt that way. Now Swayne had a clearer picture. The colonel had a better understanding of him and this field situation than he did. Yet he did not try to butt into it. He had left the decision to Swayne.

That alone made Swayne want to decide properly. For some reason, he knew he would. For now, he was not moving forward blindly, taking on the recon mission because it was there. He would not press too hard because, in his fantasy, he might see his father at the camp. Trying to do well because the colonel was there to see all the nitty-gritty that went wrong on every mission, things that could be deleted from records and reports simply by shutting off radios and video cameras. Not that it was cheating, in any case. Nobody ever sent back pictures of themselves squatting over a slit trench with their pants down around their boot tops, using the pitiful swatch of toilet paper provided in the field rations accessory kit.

All at once, Swayne saw the situation in his head as clearly as if it were spelled out for him in a plan coordinated by half a dozen staff officers. He knew what to do to make this situation work. This was not a mission to rescue his father, somebody who might not even exist. This was a mission to recon, to lay the groundwork for somebody else to pull off the rescue. For them to be safe, Swayne would have to do his job properly. The stakes were enormous. Not only the loss of life that he would have to bear on his shoulders, but also the loss of confidence in Marine Corps Force Recon, if an Army Delta Force unit attacked and was cut to ribbons because of bad information from scouts on the ground, Marine scouts from Force Recon.

Swayne knew what to do. He returned to the group and saw at once that Greiner had fixed the prisoner problem.

Greiner had cut a six-foot sapling and stripped off its branches, except for a fork at the top. He put the fork against the belly of the prisoner and tied it around his waist with a rope. Like the handle of a wagon, he could lead the man forward, or stop him by pressing back against his belly. The sapling was stout enough to support the soldier if he stumbled forward.

But even if he did fall on his face, Greiner had let the man protect himself. Greiner had tied his wrists together with a three-foot length of cord. His hands had been closed into fists and taped into place with bad-ass duct tape, so he could not grab somebody or a weapon. The cord ran behind his neck and was kept there with a rapeller's link fastened to the soldier's collar. The hookup allowed the soldier to hold both hands in front of his face to protect against twigs. He could move his hands far enough to maintain balance as he walked. If he fell, he could move one hand forward to break the fall while keeping the other one near his face. Swayne saw that somebody had put earplugs into the man's ears as well. It looked like a rig that would work.

Swayne called his group together before setting out. "Just because we started this mission off looking like the Keystone Kops is no reason it has to fall apart. Listen up. I have a couple mission changes." He explained his changes, gave his directions, and the men set off.

Swayne felt better from the new start. First, he gave the prisoner to Zavello. That would leave his team whole. He did not explain his reasons, and nobody asked about it. Even Zavello knew he did not fit into the unit's fighting scheme. He hadn't had any recent experience. He had never trained with the Spartans, did not know their tendencies, their signals, spoken or otherwise. Finally, he had lost that eye—and his depth perception.

Night Runner took up his position on point again, followed by Swayne. Zavello, using the wagon-handle expedient, followed on with the prisoner. Then came Greiner, with Friel bringing up the six.

They had lost some time, but Swayne did not regret it. They moved swiftly through the forest, and quietly. They would soon gain back what they had lost simply by regrouping. They would pull off this mission properly. And for the right reasons.

THE MONTAGNARD LEFT his companion outside the wire to guard his rifle, ammunition, and multipurpose belt. Before infiltrating the camp, he squeezed a paste of cold rice and fatty pork from a plastic bag into his mouth. He squeezed a second, equal measure of the pebbly paste into his hand, a concoction flavored with fish sauce, garlic, and onion. This he shared with his partner. He talked in low tones, revealing his plan. He would go into the camp with nothing on, not even his Old Navy underwear.

"To get through the wire, you have to feel its barbs," he said, using the language of the Montagnard, brushing rice kernels off his hands and peeling the underwear from his body. "Wait here. Stay out of trouble." He pointed at his rifle. "If I need any weapons, I'll get them inside. After I tend to business, I expect that rifle to be right where I left it." He pointed directly into the round face that stared at him intently. "You, too. Don't go anywhere unless somebody starts shooting. Then you get away and hide. I'll find you in the woods."

With that, he dropped to his knees and crawled toward the wire. He had chosen a spot not far from the main gate, where the camp road split the defenses at a double set of sally ports. Ask any of the stupid Vietnamese, and they would say the most likely area for an attempt at breaching the wire would be on the back side, the darker side of the camp. Here in front, there were more guards and more lights. The lights and each other gave the guards even more confidence that nobody would be foolish enough to try to penetrate.

The Vietnamese. They had grown so stupid. In their own war three decades go, they had scoffed at the Americans, and before them, the French, with their permanent bases. The foreigners had built up compounds and tried to protect themselves with mechanical devices. Vietcong sappers had become world experts at what he was doing now. For a while after the Americans left, the Vietnamese continued to train for such operations. Lately, though, in the last twenty years, they had become as lazy as any Western army. They no longer even trained for the skills that he was about to use on them, using only two tools.

For the first tool, he took a coil of cord about a meter long and stuffed it into the pouch of his cheek. For the second tool, he broke off a forked sapling near the ground. He put the split of the small bush into his mouth, wearing both bunches of foliage over his shoulders. Then he began his intrusion. On his hands and knees, he crawled out of the forest underbrush and across a hundred meters of cleared area among the tree trunks. With the sapling in his teeth, he smiled a little wider, a little more viciously. Because of the need to hide the camp from the air, the Vietnamese had to leave the trees in place, so their canopy would cover everything. The strong lights gave him shadows for concealment, crisscrossing avenues of approach.

Besides, as the Americans had learned with their defoliation program, the vegetation of Vietnam would not be held back. If work parties did not encircle the entire camp at least once a month, working with hoes and machetes, they could not to hope to keep it free of intrusive growth. Even that was not enough.

So, like the Americans, they had tried to fortify themselves with technology. They planted land mines near the wire and within it. Every few meters, they connected trip wires to explosives and flares. The strategy worked against them, of course. Because of all the explosive devices, nobody wanted to clear weeds and other vegetation, and even prisoners refused, preferring death by firing squad to being left to rot in the wire, crying for help, unable to get rescued because of the same fears that kept them out of the wire in the first place. So the Vietnamese had resorted to herbicides, chemicals every bit as toxic has Agent Orange. Anybody less experienced in the ways of the jungle might never see what the Montagnard had noticed even two years ago. The repeated applications of poisons, at least monthly, as near as he could tell, had eventually leached into the ground, reaching deep roots, killing the trees in stages. Already the tangled canopy above had grown sparser. Eventually, the camp would have to be moved.

He crawled like the chameleon walked. He moved an arm and a knee forward, halted a second, then moved the other arm and knee.

The Montagnard knew this was overkill. He could have stood up and walked from tree to tree, keeping in the shadows. Even if he was spotted, even if somebody shot at him, chances were good that he could escape. The trees gave cover. Most of the lights were directly on top of the towers, meaning that the shaded areas not only protected him from illumination, they also mapped out the paths safe from direct fire. He would not take a chance, though. He did not want to merely awaken the camp and escape alive. He wanted to get inside. He wanted to get to the camp's commander.

NIGHT RUNNER WONDERED what Zavello had said to Swayne when he pulled him aside. In the past, the colonel's method of counseling involved shouting and cursing enough for a rapper, body language herky-jerky, like a hip-hop dancer. Night Runner had been a victim of that himself before the last mission. Once Swayne had adjusted his plan, Runner felt better about it.

But that did not mean he felt at ease. Far from it. Night Runner had adopted the spirituality of his people. He lived it. He believed it. He loved it. Yet he did not buy into superstition. He saw no cause and effect in astrology. Rolling the dice meant knowing the odds that certain combinations added up to certain numbers in a fairly predictable sequence. Blowing on the dice made no difference. Yet he was certain that something was amiss already in this mission. It had nothing to do with their prisoner or Zavello or even Swayne's new plan.

Sometimes he believed he had a sixth sense, a psychic sense. But it was a sense, not a superstition. Sometimes he could know something without understanding it, without even knowing how or why he knew it. This sixth sense, he felt, came from his communion with nature and his spiritual world.

Yet he could not grasp it. Most times he had to divide his conscious and subconscious attentions too much between necessities of the present. He had to navigate for the team, for instance, which he could do on his body's autopilot. Once in a while, he would refer to his GPS. Once in a great while, he would refer to the topo map on his handheld computer.

For the most part, his sense of direction needed no prompting. This was not magic, as other Marines, including those on his team, often thought. When he looked at a topographic map, he memorized the contour lines. He understood them. They spoke to him, telling him the steepest part of an incline, the width of a ridge, the presence of a peak or a saddle. He counted the streams, made mental notes about how many should be flowing, according to the map symbol, and how many should be dried gullies. He paid attention to the colors, understood where he would expect to find deep vegetation, where trees had been logged, where undergrowth was thin. Then, as he walked, he put that mental computer of his to work, subconsciously counting paces, consciously ticking off the landmarks rather than aimlessly walking. He could go through a dense forest without circling, the natural tendency. He would pick a tree ten meters ahead or fifty meters ahead, whatever the thickness of the growth would give him. Before he got there, he would line up a tree in the distance on the same line. Over and over with regularity and accuracy, he would keep up this line. Then, at stops, he would check his GPS, make a mental correction, and when he set out again, adjust his course. No magic to it.

Even so, these things required part of his concentration. He also had to inventory his senses the way a helicopter pilot inventories the instrument panel at a glance, at least once a minute. As experienced as he was, he had to remind himself to taste the air like the rattlesnake. He forced himself to record the feeling of the breeze against his cheek, against the back of his hand. Every few breaths, he inhaled deeply through his nose, sorting the smells, remembering them. Comparing them to all the odors he had collected in the previous hour. Even his senses of sight and hearing—those that most men relied on alone—he exercised with deliberate care.

He had learned to form individual compartments for his hearing. The noise of his mates, the occasional stumbling of

Greiner and Friel, the regularity of the footsteps of the captain. These he wrote into the background texture of his hearing. Sometimes, when he exerted himself, he could hear not only his breathing and his pulse but also the coursing of his blood through his veins. Again, he put these things into the background of his hearing, using them as a basis for listening. Anything that deviated from the baseline, he paid attention to. Nothing did he take for granted. If a twig fell from a branch, he wanted to understand why. He would focus his hearing on the spot, then upward, trying to locate an animal. Calling on his other senses to assist, he listened for the hum of a breeze blowing over a trip wire, a misstep by an enemy.

His vision, with or without binoculars and night vision devices, he used unlike most people.

He borrowed from the elk and the deer, whose hearing and sight were nothing, if not spectacular. They were the masters of background comparisons. They could lift their head and stare ahead, swiveling their ears in all directions, including behind them. Most often they stared downwind. Their noses then came into play, telling them of the approach of the wolf, the lion, the bear, or the hunter on two legs, from behind.

When he had first started tracking as a boy, he would walk into the foothills of the Rockies to the west of Heart Butte, Montana. He would knot a bristly headband of the sweet grass in the grassy foothills. In the forest, he would weave himself a simple camouflaged hat of pine boughs. He would creep up every incline a step at a time, searching the landscape that he could see beyond until he spotted the mule deer or the great Rocky Mountain elk. With only his eyes showing beneath his camo, he would survey the landscape. Then he would lie down and creep forward on his belly until the animals again came into view. For hours he would watch them browsing the forest or grazing the meadows on the slopes.

From these elk and deer, the prey animals, he learned how to move and hunt and how to elude the hunter.

He learned that the elk would inventory the area around itself each time it moved. He decided the animal was recording the position of everything, living or dead. Then, if it checked a second time from the same vantage point, all it had to do was compare it to the picture in its short-term memory, looking for differences, changes, new threats. Even if he was wrong in the details of his surmise, the conclusion made sense, so he taught himself the technique. In order to never have to look at a landscape a second time as if it were new, he never tried to take in everything with each glance. He had already memorized everything. All he had to do was confirm what he had seen the first time and look for changes.

He learned to walk through the forest like the elk, too. In times of danger, take one step or two, then freeze. This worked two ways. First, it made his motion a blur. Any other predator in motion, especially a man, had very little chance of seeing the movement. Even if he were spotted, the next, frozen moment gave the elk the best chance of going undetected. At times when he needed to move more quickly, to cover ground, the elk walked slowly, gracefully, deliberately. Then, although the chances for detection were higher, the graceful pace also helped in keeping its head from bouncing, allowing the elk a better chance of seeing a threat while on the move. Night Runner behaved like the lead cow in an elk herd, walking slowly, keeping his head from bobbing or weaving, halting often to check in all directions.

He found so much more to learn from the prey than the predator. The bear, for instance, was more a gatherer than a hunter. He took food where he found it and seldom stalked his quarry. If the bear happened upon an animal it might turn into a meal, it charged, boldly, powerfully, running down its meal in a burst of speed. If necessary, it could maintain that speed as fast as a horse, for longer than most horses. But usually, it did not hunt like the cheetah, using speed and endurance; that was too costly in terms of burning precious calories needed for the winter sleep.

The wolf, hunting in packs, was more suited to that. It hunted boldly, too. Usually without stealth, the pack went after its prey, hunting in turn at the lead, breaking trail in the snow for the other wolves.

The eagles and other soaring birds could take a vantage point above, using their fantastic eyesight to spot prey, then dive into the attack from the sky. The Air Force had learned this technique and used it still, with the extraordinary improvement that a Force Recon Marine could find the target and illuminate it with a laser beam so the soaring bomber could strike without even the dive or the need to see its prey.

Not even the great cats of the Rocky Mountains were a good study subject for learning how to hunt and strike. For the cougar had never learned to fear. It could walk around the forest unconcerned. At the top of the food chain, no other creature hunted it. It could lie in ambush. It could stalk. It could rush. It could leap. But, as a rule, it could never know the fear of the elk or deer.

So Night Runner had learned from the prey animal, which had to stay vigilant every hour of its tenuous life. From the elk he had developed his senses—all six of them—and most important, the realization that he could never let down his guard. Ever.

So, by the time he had led his team through the forest on its first leg of the journey and arrived at the dark and dangerous Ho Chi Minh Trail, he knew that something was wrong. More than one of his senses had confirmed it: something was stalking the Spartans.

"Spartan One, this is Two, Charlie Papa Xray," he reported, telling the others that he had identified Checkpoint Xray, where the first leg of their route hit the Ho Chi Minh Trail. According to Swayne's plan, they would hold the position, keeping all-round security, while Night Runner reconned the trail in both directions to see if there were any patrols or vehicle traffic. Their route had taken them more than four kilometers south of the destroyed missile and refueling site, so there was some danger of local security and cleanup crews passing by.

SWAYNE SENSED THAT something was wrong the moment that Night Runner called him forward. They shut off their mikes at the same moment without the need for a word or a signal.

Night Runner jerked a thumb over his shoulder. "The trail's right behind me, maybe fifty meters."

Swayne looked. "I don't see anything. How do you know?"

"The vegetation above the trail. Patterns of soot, dying foliage. From the diesel exhaust of passing trucks."

Swayne nodded, looked again, then shook his head. "I still don't see anything." The tone of his voice deepened. "What else?"

Night Runner told him his suspicions. Swayne did not ask for proof. He did not even ask the gunny to tell him which elements on the hour-long march had tipped him off. If Night Runner had identified a threat, Swayne needed to know only one thing: "How do we deal with it?"

Night Runner said, "Suppose I make a circuit around Xray? If I give you an all clear, you lead the others down the superhighway to Yankee, move off into the jungle, and wait for me to let you know what the next move ought to be. I'll keep to the forest and watch your six."

Swayne nodded once. "I'll tell the others." As he turned on his microphone and lifted his head, all he could see in his night vision binoculars was the empty space where Night Runner had been. He turned his head quickly in both directions, his vision a blur, trying to catch a glimpse of Runner leaving the position. He could not even find a sign of trembling foliage to indicate where the man had been.

"Stop moving your head so quickly," Night Runner's voice said into his earpiece. "Now turn slowly. Slowly. Now stop. Do you see me?"

Swayne shook his head, knowing that Runner must be looking right at him.

"Go to IR."

Swayne switched his goggles from the night vision mode, which amplified existing light, creating images as good as an ordinary wide-screen television, with the colors muted. When he switched to infrared, the goggles gave a much less defined picture, tinged in nuclear-glow green, the hotter the thermal image, the brighter the color. Two bright spots showed up immediately, barely five meters away. Night Runner stood facing him. The specially treated fabric in his uniform deflected and diffused his body heat so it did not show up to IR detection devices. Vents in the clothing directed heat to the back of his uniform, making him less likely to be seen by an enemy head-on.

Gradually the picture came into view. Night Runner stood facing him, his side pressed into the trunk of a tree. A horizontal branch came off the tree at about his eye level. Runner had propped his arm on top of the branch and elevated it slightly, so it looked like a limb of the tree and not his own body. He was looking at Swayne between his fingers, holding a clump of foliage in front of his face to break up the outline of his head. He held his other arm close to his body, bent at the elbow so the forearm and hand projected like a branch. The only giveaways were thermal ones, both his hands glowing bright. If he had worn his IR-scattering gloves, Swayne might not yet have seen him yet. Night Runner waved his fingers, ducked behind the tree trunk, and was gone for good.

Swayne briefed his troops over the radio on his change of plans. Before he had finished, he realized that Night Runner had not merely been playing a game of hide-and-seek with him a moment ago. He was sending him a message, demonstrating how to look for the enemy stalking them. The night vision mode of their goggles made a walk through the woods seem like a simple daylight hike, allowing troops near-perfect depth of vision and the ability to see fine details. But the nearly monochromatic landscape hid things from them, too. Night Runner had been suggesting, at least for the walk on the new Ho Chi Minh Trail, the Spartans should use the other mode.

"Switch to IR mode on your binoculars," he ordered. Then, to spare Zavello the embarrassment of asking, he stepped up to the colonel's side to help him find the switch and make the adjustment.

THE MONTAGNARD HAD studied this camp for three months four years ago. Every year since, he had come back to lie and watch from the forest, to confirm what he had learned in his first study, to adjust his thinking and learn new tricks during a week of refresher study.

What he had found was a security force growing more lax every year. They supposed that they could afford to relax. After all, the inmates kept getting older. Soon they would die out. In the last year alone the numbers had dropped by almost one-fourth. Each year, one of his tests had been to capture rats. He would let his companion terrorize them, then set them loose so they would run away toward the camp. If the guards ever saw the scurrying animals at all, it was in that first stretch of relatively open ground between the undergrowth and the wire. Once the animal got into the wire, no matter how brightly it was lit, the guards seldom saw it until it broke under the last barrier and ran onto the grounds. Since the Montagnard knew the tendency, he was certain he could exploit it.

He crawled to the first obstacle, a grid of barbed wire strands woven in diamond shapes, the netting held six inches off the ground, attached to the tops of metal spikes. The Montagnard already knew this area had not been protected by mines or booby traps; work parties used hoes to chop vegetation that grew up through the eight-inch diamonds.

The herbicides were only used in areas where men could not safely walk. No longer needing the camouflage, he took his forked branch from his mouth and broke off the foliage, keeping the part that looked like a bird's wishbone for later. This he carried in his teeth.

The Montagnard took the first part of the obstacle in seconds, rolling over onto his back, burrowing into the earth softened by hoes, and slithering beneath the wire. When a barb tried to impale him, he lifted the wire with one finger or exhaled or shifted a muscle. At any one time he might be touching the wire in half a dozen places. It did not matter to the Montagnard. Each part of his body seemed capable of operating with its own solution to the barbs, and he was at the first roll of concertina in no time. He removed the length of cord from his mouth and used it to tie his genitalia deep into his groin, wearing the loose ends like a thong knotted at the small of his back and tied into a belt around his waist.

The secret to dealing with concertina was not to fight the thousands of blades tipped at both ends with needle points. Concertina had to be caressed, seduced. The Vietnamese had been careless in deploying the coils of this first row, which lay like a Slinky toy around the entire camp. They had staked down the coils, but too far apart. He went for a spot at the midpoint between two stakes. When his hair snagged in the wire, he took the fork stuck from his mouth and used it to lift the roll, continuing to slither along with barely a pause. He only had to lift the coils a few inches, because his body was so flat. Once his belly button had cleared, he sat up partially, rolled to his side, still keeping the wire suspended with the forked stick, and rotated his legs clear. He now lay in a space barely a foot wide where the next obstacle began. There the difficulty increased. The Vietnamese had built a tent frame of barbed wire, putting a line of poles six feet tall completely around the camp. A strand of barbed wire ran from pole to pole like the ridge of the tent. Strands of wire then hung off the ridgepole, crisscrossing outward from the centerline to a distance of ten meters. Besides keeping sappers out, the first three lines of obstacles were intended to prevent an attack on the more formidable barriers that still lay between the Montagnard and the camp. The stacked rolls of concertina, the chain link fence, the mines, booby traps, and flares.

To crawl through the sloping network of wires, the Montagnard made himself into a four-legged spider. Keeping his torso just a foot off the ground, he worked his arms and legs slowly, feeling for trip wires, supporting his body as he wormed through a hole between wires. The interior of a wire tent was crisscrossed by random lines leading to booby traps and flares. If he were to touch off one of the white phosphorus devices by pulling the pin, machine guns at the two nearest towers would open up on the area without waiting to identify a target. One of his rats had just done just such thing earlier in the year. The flare cast frightful shadows, making the rodent seem a grotesque horse rather than the small dog that it was.

But the Montagnard also knew something about the trip wires connected to the flares and grenades. To keep the rats from setting off more devices, the Vietnamese had bent over the ends of the grenade pins so it took a strong pressure to set off the flare. Long ago perhaps, the security force had used the push-pull type releases, a spring-loaded pin that could either be pulled out to set off the grenade or, if a taut wire was cut, the spring device would set it off, too. Too many false alarms—falling branches, and even heavy breezes—had set off the more sensitive devices. Now only a falling branch or an especially clumsy person—perhaps a prisoner smacking it with a weed cutter—could set one off.

The Montagnard continued moving like a spider, putting each hand and foot down gingerly, searching for the telltale pressure plate of a land mine.

As he went, he wondered whether the American Indian of the Force Recon team would be able to move as well. He would like to have had a competition between himself and the man. He felt superior to him, certain that he had not had the kind of experience that the Montagnard was now using. In their trips to the forest to the refueling site to destroy the missile, he had seen moments of hesitation. The American had relied on his technology instead of his natural abilities, of which he had many. That reliance made him a weaker man, for the technologies would never be able to accomplish what the body of a full-time jungle warrior could do. Technology gave a human too many unfiltered sensations. Too much information at once, information not sorted and evaluated. In years of living in the forest with the animals, the Montagnard had come to understand the creatures and their ways. This gave him his edge.

The Montagnard relied on his sensations, while the American relied on circuits and transistors and electricity. Besides, the American, no matter how many combat missions he had fought, had spent barely a fraction of his life in battle. No matter how realistic his training, he could not know what the Montagnard had been through. At the age of nine he became a man, after he killed his first enemy, a French soldier who mistook him for one of the Vietminh near Dien Bien Phu. Since then, many of his enemies had died at his hands, including countless Vietnamese, his traditional enemies. But he had many enemies: people who tried to incorporate him into a foreign culture; Cambodians from the Pol Pot regime; Laotians; men of every nationality, if they insulted him; men by the hundreds that he had been paid to kill.

NIGHT RUNNER ALLOWED himself a brief smile after he heard Swayne give the order for the team to go to IR mode. Walking down the road would no longer present problems of avoiding fallen timber, everything from stacks of twigs to deadfalls of mature trees. The team would no longer have to worry about falling into a gully, anything in size from an ankle-buster to a mini–Death Valley hidden by the undergrowth.

He made a swift, silent sweep around the team position, circling counterclockwise and keeping a distance of about fifty meters, so they could not spot him through the forest and be alarmed. He was not so worried that they would snap off a reckless shot. The team was too disciplined to do that when they knew that he was in the area. He could not be so sure about Zavello, not having worked with him in the field.

As he completed the circuit, he stretched the distance between himself and the team before crossing the Ho Chi Minh Trail, a hard-packed dirt surface just wide enough for the one-way traffic of a large truck. He remembered seeing the horizontal scratches on the sides of the tractor trailer carrying the missile. Now he knew why. Once away from larger cleared-out areas like the refueling site, the truck had to navigate through a tunnel in the jungle as tight as a bore brush down the barrel of a rifle.

He picked a spot just five meters across the trail, where a depression would allow him to lie down. He stepped away from the position he had chosen and tore off several small green branches from a bush. He lay down in the low spot and replanted the foliage in front of his face, leaving enough space for his eyes so he could watch the road. Before making a call to Swayne to let him know it was safe to move out, he waited a moment. He wanted to let the sensations and impressions of the past fifteen minutes soak in. He wanted to bounce one off the other, seeing if he could strike a spark of recognition that would help him understand what was wrong.

For surely something was out of place. Some things were easy. Two nights ago, the Montagnard had given him a complete rundown on traffic flow over this secret superhighway. Last night, before the attack, he had seen proof of what the Montagnard told him. Occasional patrols on bicycles and motorcycles, usually two armed soldiers, usually driving slowly because of their low-power, hooded night-driving lamps. One or two light trucks an hour, probably couriers or supply vehicles. Then the missile carrier and its security vehicles. So far tonight, he had seen nothing. Of course, that might mean nothing. Today's battle in the jungle between two Vietnamese units. The apparent escape of the invaders. The fire and destruction at the refueling site. Quite possibly nobody was running around like chickens with their heads cut off because their heads had in fact rolled.

Then there was the forest, too quiet to suit him. Perhaps the battle. Perhaps the Americans moving through it, although that did not seem likely. A forest should have been more noisy, the animals expressing their outrage at being disturbed by the scent, sight, and sound of humans.

Finally, there was the—

"Spartan Two, this is One. Status, over."

Night Runner felt a moment of embarrassment for not getting back to the captain sooner. "This is Two. Area clear. You're good to go. The only thing I could find was—"

Night Runner bit his lower lip. He had to tell them of the danger. "The only thing I could find was the sign of a tiger."

Friel spoke up first, out of turn. "Whoa! Chief, did you say tiger?"

"You saw a tiger?" said Zavello, demanding an answer to a question he had no business asking.

"Clear this net," Swayne said, a respectful way of telling everybody to shut up. "No more chatter. Speak only if you have a tactical reason. Can we move out?"

Night Runner couldn't help smiling. Swayne himself had shut up, waiting for him to speak up. Because he had said he found the sign of a tiger, Swayne accepted it. It didn't matter whether he reported seeing one—which he had not— or smelling it, which he did. If Night Runner said there was a tiger out there, there was a tiger.

"It was close to our formation and recently, but it has moved away. You are clear to move out."

Night Runner watched as they went by a few minutes later. Completely in defilade, he could see them coming down the trail. As they neared, he ducked out of sight so they could not pick up the thermal signature of his eyes, so the team could not mistake them for those of a huge cat.

After they passed, he watched them disappear around a bend in the foliage tunnel. It did not surprise him to see Force Recon Marines staying alert as they moved in a tactical formation. But he had never seen Marines being *so* careful. He could not help noticing that they had tightened up their marching interval, Friel practically walking on Greiner's heels, when he should have allowed a minimum of five meters—the killing radius of a bursting grenade—and maybe twice that much between himself and the man he was following.

He remained in position for a full ten minutes, wanting to be certain that neither man nor beast would follow his team.

Except for that brief moment ten minutes ago when the rancid, musty smell of the tiger stung his nose, he had no further clues that the animal was still stalking the Spartans.

He waited a full twenty minutes to be sure. Then he set out after them, working his way through the forest. He stayed close to the road, though, so he could sound a warning if he spotted any Vietnamese motor—or cat—traffic closing on them from the rear.

On his way through the maze of the wire tent, the Montagnard changed directions, looking for a particular spot in the next part of the defenses, the coiled pyramid. The Vietnamese engineers had built a traditional barbed wire fence, except eight feet tall with seven strands. On either side, snaking around the camp, the engineers had laid three coils of concertina on the ground. On top of that they had stacked two coils, again anchoring them to the central wire fence. At the next level a single layer on each side was tied to the barbed wire strands. On top of the posts, going all way around again, was a single strand of coils.

But somebody had tried to do the job on the cheap. To

conserve money, they had squandered their precious coin of security. They had cheated on these layers of coils. Every other coil had been stretched a few extra feet, leaving spaces at the attachment points among the coils. They were only four-inch spaces, to be sure, but it was a virtual open-door policy for the Montagnard. The engineers had been clever enough to alternate a stretched length with a loose one in successive concentric rings. At one spot, parts of loose coils lined up, creating a superhighway through the fences. Using his spider technique, he turned, twisted, and snaked his body like a dancing mime through the bottom coils and the barbed wire strands, barely touching the concertina, let alone getting snagged on it.

Another stretch of netting with its diamond holes lay ahead of him, four inches off the ground. He went through it like a flat worm, changing directions to reach the point where he would enter the camp through its last barrier, the ten-foot chain-link fence topped by an inverted pyramid of concertina coils. He aimed for the spot where rainfall had piled trash against the base of the fence, the normal flotsam and jetsam of the rainy season, which had barely begun.

He wasn't interested in the trash so much, although it would give him some concealment. If water had flowed there, it would yield something more important.

Beneath the trash he found what he wanted. The architects had built a concrete open-drainage system for the camp, something able to carry off the torrents of water that fell during the monsoon season. So much water had run through the fence at this point that it had worn down the concrete nearly a full inch. So much trash had piled against the fence during the runoff that the wire mesh had stretched out of shape like a wet wool sweater. He found a gap of three inches between the fence and the concrete drain, wide enough for him to lie on his back. It was more than enough space. With his head against the sharp edges of the bottom hem of the fence, he curled the edge up with both hands, finding an extra two inches, slithering through like a baby being born. Then he rolled on his stomach, his ankles still under the wire, and draped a piece of cardboard over part of his body. A few seconds of listening, smelling, and feeling for vibrations through his chest on the ground told him nobody had sounded the alarm. So he inched across the deadline—ten feet of cleared ground behind a knee-high barrier, so named because if any prisoner walked into that area without permission, he could be shot dead on sight. Finally he found himself in the shadows of a stucco building roofed with red tiles in the style of French plantation architecture. He stood up and dusted himself off quietly. A quick check of his mental stopwatch told him that he had made it through in just a few ticks over three minutes. Nobody—nobody in the world, including the American Indian—could have breached the camp walls so quickly.

The rest was easy. At a full two hours before dawn, the garrison, including the inmates, would be sleeping their soundest, concerned more with bundling up against the chill than anything else. He knew the layout of the camp from his previous visits and recons. He simply kept to the shadows until he found the commandant's quarters. The camp buildings were built on stilts to keep the floors dry during the monsoon floods. He crawled beneath the commandant's. He lay still for a long time beneath the colonel's bedroom. He listened for the sound of breathing. What he heard was weeping. On the opposite side of the building, he stood up and slipped open a window screen, going over the windowsill like a black curtain being dragged inside. He walked past a dozing guard, not even bothering to take his weapon. If he needed to, he had enough power in his bare hands to deal with the commandant.

He found the doorknob, turned it, and stepped inside, surprised to find a burning candle and wisps of incense floating up from a small shrine against the wall. The colonel, on his knees before the candles, sensed his presence. The Montagnard saw the wavering of the stream of rising incense smoke and realized that a breeze stirred up by opening the door must have given him away.

"What took you so long?" asked the colonel in French.

"I'm early—because I took a shortcut around your incessant red tape. What gave me away?"

"Your smell."

"Garlic."

"Where's your friend?"

"Outside the wire. He gets edgy around your men. Besides, he's not so clever about getting through the wire as I am." An awkward pause followed. "You're upset."

The colonel lowered his head suddenly, as if he had forgotten for a moment. Puddled tears fell to the floor. "My son. He died. From his burns."

The colonel raised his head a little, eyes looking out from beneath his dark brow. "What news?"

"You shall have your revenge," said the Montagnard in fluent Vietnamese. "The Americans are coming."

The Montagnard revealed all that he knew. The colonel asked no questions until the naked man stood up.

"Where are you going?"

"Back into the jungle, where it is safer. They are coming here, perhaps to spy on you, perhaps to attack. Either way, I should not be seen with you."

The colonel's grief had begun its shift to anger. "I will kill them, but first I need information," he said, his tone cold and deliberate. "I will pay you handsomely."

"Of course you will. In gold."

"In gold. The more precious the information, the heavier the payment."

The Montagnard loosed a wide smile. "I will bring you back something more valuable than its weight in gold. I will bring you another American for your collection, for your revenge."

• • •

SWAYNE SETTLED THE team into a tight perimeter a full fifty meters off the road and just east of Checkpoint Yankee. He sent a one-word message over the radio to let Night Runner know they had arrived: "Yankee."

"Roger, Yankee. I'll be coming in from your . . . zero-five-five degrees."

Swayne had long ago stopped asking how Night Runner could do things like that. They had walked in the clear, practically at double time, along the roads smooth and level enough for bowling. Somehow Night Runner had bypassed them, wending his way through the tangle of the jungle, and was coming at them from the front. Swayne turned to the azimuth that Night Runner had given him, the digits visible on the heads-up display of his night vision goggles. Two hot spots of green showed up, dead on in his field of view. Night Runner had lifted up his goggles from the hinged headband. He walked in, his rifle in one hand, his open palm exposed, hot to the night vision devices, in the other.

Swayne and Night Runner put their heads together, literally, and shut off their microphones.

"Well," said Swayne, "I have to ask the billion-dollar question that's on everybody else's mind."

"The tiger? No sign of it. Nothing followed us. And there's nothing within one hundred meters of this spot, either. I already checked it out."

Night Runner smiled broadly, the back of his mouth showing extra hot in Swayne's goggles. "I notice everybody seems on max alert tonight."

"You didn't make up the tiger, did you? Just to keep everybody on their toes?"

"No, but I was thinking, when I saw the team go past, that it might not be a bad idea in the future. A kind of invisible motivation."

Swayne tried to suppress a laugh but couldn't avoid snorting. "I have to admit, it got to me. I must have told myself a dozen times to stop worrying about a tiger. What we have to worry about are men. Hundreds, maybe thousands of men might be within a few miles of here, all of them armed with RPGs and rifles. You mention the word *tiger*, and everybody in the unit is terrified, except for the Vietnamese soldier. That's how I know he can't speak English, by the way."

"How much longer do you want to rest?" Night Runner asked.

Swayne checked the time on his heads-up display. "Let's go. We can settle in, pound down some carbs, and catch a couple hours' sleep once we get within striking distance of the camp."

They arrived at Zulu two hours later. Swayne rejected the spot he had originally chosen as a staging area, a series of gentle hills with a river cutting steep banks to the east. On the map, the ground would give them plenty of room to escape to the north. The bluffs would shield them from the east. Once in the area, though, he saw that the forest floor had been beaten down with foot traffic like a public playground. Either the Vietnamese used the area as a training ground hidden from the prying eyes of satellites, or else the enemy's soldiers patrolled the area continually. Night Runner was glad for Swayne's decision. He would have rejected the area because of the faint but fresh odor of the tiger.

Nobody else in the group remarked on the smell. Maybe because they thought it came from the camp. Maybe they hadn't sat close enough at the circus. He didn't bring it up.

Swayne directed him to a secondary position, farther up the slope. The landscape became wild again, and Night Runner led them to a saddle between two of the hills. They crossed over and settled into a crease in the ground. *Much better*. The move put them on the side of the high ground away from the camp. They could approach by walking around the summit of the hill to find the camp below them.

Night Runner wanted to go out on his own right away.

"No," Swayne said. "We have four hours. I'm going to put the colonel on guard duty for all of it. Then each of us is going to take an hour-long turn on watch so he can rest. I'm leaving him behind to guard the prisoner."

Night Runner didn't see any wiggle room in the way Swayne put it, but he asked anyhow. "I couldn't use my watch to make a recce?"

"No. I want the colonel rested. I want you rested."

The captain had a point. It would not hurt to be refreshed before moving out more than an hour before dawn in recon groups of two. His team needed him to be fresh.

So the Spartans settled in, trying to restore their tired, sweating bodies, as the cold crept out of the night, trying to keep them awake and exhaust them by making their muscles tremble against the chill.

"The hawk is out," Zavello said, after Swayne briefed him.

Swayne cocked his head. "Sir?"

"Never mind."

Swayne figured the saying was another relic of Vietnam past.

SPARTAN STAGING AREA, VIETNAM
12APR02—0423 HOURS LOCAL

SWAYNE HAD ONLY rarely felt the kind of push-pull that he had been going through on the last hour as they moved out of their staging area. Tactically, he didn't like the idea that they would have to move so close to the camp to be able to see anything. Watching from the high ground was out of the question for the same reason that satellites could not see anything: the canopy. No question, they had to get close. Emotionally, he did not want to deal with the hope— or the fear—that his father might be in this camp. He hadn't exactly buried Jack Swayne Sr. Since nobody had brought the remains home, he literally could not do that. Just because the Defense Department presumed that he was dead did not make it so. The mistakes of bureaucrats were legion. This could just be another. So, in his mind, he had put his father somewhere between the image of a pile of scattered bones gnawed to nothing by rodents in the jungle and the photo of a stiff-backed young Marine in dress whites that he kept buried in a footlocker at his apartment. Probably closer to the rodents, he had always figured. Now this.

Hell, he had never even allowed himself to think that his father might be held a prisoner of war. He had read the stories of Aleksandr Solzhenitsyn. At least part of them. Never could he finish one that had to do with the Gulag. Now, if the intelligence people—more bureaucrats—were right, he was about to look in on a warm-weather version of the archipelago.

His plan was simple and flexible, the best kind. He had drawn three goose eggs on the screen of his PDA. He and Greiner would navigate to a spot within the first goose egg from which they could see without being seen. Runner and Friel would split off and occupy a second goose egg to recon from a separate point of view. Once in position, both teams would take pictures, showing the layout of the camp, especially to confirm the presence and location of American MIAs. They would try to get a feeling for the routine of the camp, but especially to confirm or deny the presence of POWs. If the finding was negative, both could leave, pull back to their third goose egg, a rally point, and be extracted. If confirmed, PaCom would put together a mission from Delta Force to pull the prisoners out.

Both teams would borrow from the Vietcong, setting up booby traps along their withdrawal trails to delay and harass any enemy forces that tried to pursue them.

Swayne always felt uneasy about navigating through forests and jungles on his own. He had all the technological devices: the night vision goggles, the heads-up GPS. In theory, he could navigate through this jungle at night as easily as taking a walk in the park in broad daylight. He had already preprogrammed his GPS package to get him to his destination. An arrow pointed directly at it in the heads-up display. All he had to do was follow the arrow until it reversed itself. In theory, he would be within half a meter of his destination.

But theory, especially when coupled with technology, didn't always reflect reality. Following an arrow seemed simple until you added a jungle, rivers, and deadfalls. He had to focus on walking and seeing as well as navigating. All those activities at once tended to make a man lose sight of the tactical imperatives. They had an enemy to worry about on top of everything else. Not to mention poisonous snakes and insects. And now, tigers. Likewise, Force Recon's night vision goggles were certainly a vast improvement over previous versions of night observation devices, NODs. The NOD had two eyepieces that formed a single image from a monocular epicenter of the wearer's face. The image tended to be flat and confined to a circle, like looking through the tube of a toilet paper roll. The viewer had no depth of vision, no sense of distance, and no ability to see danger from the side. Whereas the night vision binoculars gave a panoramic view, true binocular vision that allowed the user to run and fight in them. But they still reduced the field of view, and the image could be washed out by a bright light, say, the muzzle flash of a rifle.

When Swayne was still a kilometer from his goose egg, Night Runner reported that he and Friel had established themselves in position, finding an observation post that gave him a clear, elevated view of the camp.

"Roger," Swayne said. *Elevated? How could that be?*

He adjusted the view selections inside his receiver pack, allowing his binoculars to project any video transmitted by Night Runner inside the barrels of the NVGs. He called a halt. Greiner stepped away from their line of travel and turned back to look toward the rear. Swayne was proud of the young corporal. He made very few mistakes. Those he did make he never repeated.

The video image told him at once what Night Runner meant about being elevated. Of course, he had climbed a tree.

• • •

ZAVELLO HAD ALREADY made peace with his mission of pulling guard. He knew it was the only way he could be useful. He had come to Vietnam on an impulse, a dumb-ass impulse at that. He didn't need the bone-rattling dampness to tell him that. He didn't need the cramps that migrated from his calves to his hamstrings to his buttocks to remind him that he was over the hill. Nobody in the Marine Corps his age could have been in better shape for jogging back and forth on a level beach in his bare feet. Or at running foam-padded, air-cushioned soles around the asphalt-paved tracks built for the purpose on the base. But just one day of humping the hills with a weapon and a pack told him that combat conditioning was another matter. The change in schedule. The change in rations. All those things . . .

Bullshit, he told himself. It wasn't the training. It was the age.

Bullshit again, he told himself. He had lost it. Look at Monty, a man older even than himself. He had not lost a step over the years. Because he lived at the edge of danger all of his life, whereas Zavello had only left the comfort of a military base to visit danger for short periods. He didn't belong.

He had lost more than a step. He had lost his edge. When his prisoner began to shiver, he had taken off his own heat-reflective poncho and wrapped it around the young man, who sat squatting on his heels. Christ, he hoped none of the bird colonels and generals back at the Pentagon ever found out. He might never recover from the damage to his reputation.

Zavello then was left to shiver. He tried walking around awhile, keeping the cramps worked out. Then he thought he might sit on his heels the way the Vietnamese did. His knees barely unlocked after just ten minutes of squatting. He had to be up, he had to stay moving.

He had a duty, however trivial, and although it might be beneath a full-bird Marine colonel to be guarding a Vietnamese soldier who couldn't have been more than eighteen years old and scared to death, it was his job, his combat mission.

Funny thing. Because he had put himself on the ground, he had, in effect, surrendered his position of authority. Because of the combat experience, every member of the Spartan team had a right to direct him in case things got hot. Even the corporal, the Greiner kid. He had recent combat experience. He knew how to use the high-tech equipment. He had current training. He had been in the shit more in the last year and a half than Zavello had been in the last thirty.

Not funny. Zavello realized that among all the other things that he had lost was his ability to foresee such an obvious outcome of going to the field in a place where he didn't belong. Hell, even though the Marines had sent him over here as a young fire-eating lieutenant, he didn't belong now.

He was not merely standing in a fog, he was living in one. He—

"Christ." The fog had grown hot for a second. It had grown strong with a stench of urine, of musk, of the rancid breath of a dragon.

SWAYNE WATCHED AS the video recorder in Night Runner's rifle scope swept the camp. He ignored Zavello's one-word outburst in his open mike. All he needed to know was that things were still quiet inside the wire. He might need a full half-hour more than Night Runner to get into position. Satisfied, he wiped the video from his display.

With a word to Greiner, he made yet another check of the forest ahead of him and stepped out, detouring past their rally point. One thing he wanted to see inside their third goose egg was a soccer field–sized clearing in the forest only a quarter mile from the camp. Nothing would obstruct a helicopter landing, as far as he could see. The tall grass and fog had formed in the undisturbed meadow, creating an eerie sight in his night vision goggles. Swayne needed to know if that would be a suitable place to put down special operations aircraft for the attack and the rescue mission. The spot was

the only place for miles that offered hope of landing helicopters. Attackers could rappel down ropes, but choppers
would have to set down to take on prisoners rescued from
the Vietnamese. Same for Zavello and the Vietnamese prisoner.

Zavello. He wondered how the old man was doing. Before
the two teams of Spartans had pulled out of the staging area,
he overheard Zavello grumbling, bitching about being as
worthless as tits on a bull. Swayne thought it was funny in
one sense. The colonel had come out to the field with the
idea that he could get a feel for the action. He would have
had more information back at his desk inside the OMCC,
where he could have radio intercepts on demand, access to
satellite images, video from the battlefield, and secure land-
lines to Delta Force before the rescue operation, and a bot-
tomless cup of hot coffee besides. As it was, he had nothing
but a case of the chills and the job of a private, standing
guard over the Vietnamese prisoner. When they had left him
back at the staging area, Zavello was spooning a cold ration
of pasta to the man, who was unable to feed himself because
his fingers were immobilized with bad-ass duct tape. Swayne
wondered how the colonel would handle his charge when the
man needed to pee. That he'd pay to see.

ZAVELLO KNEW THE smell. He had been to the circus. He
had watched the big cats. Now he knew he was smelling
one. Nearby. No doubt, it was smelling him as well.

He turned his rifle, then his body. He crouched, feeling
for the safety on his CAR-15. He shifted the selection lever
from safe, past single shot, to full auto.

He had left his night vision binoculars in the thermal-
sensing mode, just as Swayne had told him and the others
to do. But the fog, cold and clinging as a wet blanket,
shrouded his vision.

Zavello fought panic, the urge to shoot into the fog, spray-
ing bullets upwind, into the smell, hoping for a lucky shot,

wanting to make some noise to drive the animal away if he could not kill it.

He wiped a sleeve across the wraparound lens of his binoculars. He left a smear of mud and could not bite back a curse for such a stupid move. He tore at the knot in the camo bandanna around his neck.

Robbed of his sense of sight, the panic grew. He knew his hearing was not all that good on the best of days. The only thing working was his sense of smell. Even his sense of touch was gone, replaced by trembles and numbness.

He had put himself into this position and had come to the conclusion that he did not belong. That was bad enough. If he ever got out of this alive, he had worried that he might never live down pulling off such a cowboy stunt. Never mind the generals that would chew his ass. He had plenty of buddies who would never give him a rest for such a John Wayne move.

But forget about those fears. Now his choices in life had been reduced to two. If he fired his rifle blindly into the fog, he might kill the stalking tiger, but he would ruin the mission. He would endanger the lives of the four men who had gone down to be close to the camp.

If he did not shoot, he might lose his life. In a place where he did not belong. Trying to pull off something he had no business trying.

His damp bandanna, when it finally came free of his neck, helped some. It cleared the smear and the mist from the lens of his night vision goggles.

He realized the hot scent had been replaced by the cold, dank smell of the forest.

He felt an instant of relief. Not only that the tiger had left but also that he had not shot his rifle in panic. He took his finger out of the trigger guard so he would not touch off a round by accident. He did not put the rifle to safe. That would be stupid. If the tiger attacked, he would shoot it. If necessary, he had always thought that he would give his life for his country. Of course, that did not include committing suicide. Nowhere in his oath did it say that he would have to turn himself into a cable laid in a box of kitty litter to be honorable.

He turned toward his prisoner.

The kid had smelled it, too. He had laid himself out on the ground.

No! A newer, hotter image had made the horizontal hot green slash on his thermal display screen.

Like a horrific image from reality television, the huge animal straddled the Vietnamese prisoner, the man's head in its mouth. As he watched, the tiger shut its jaws, and the head disappeared into the maw. Zavello heard the crunch, like somebody biting into a stalk of celery.

SWAYNE SAW TWO indistinct bright spots of light in the skies ahead of him. One he knew to be the first suggestion of sunrise on the eastern horizon. Because he could see the sky at all, he knew he had reached the clearing. One problem had plagued him all along the way. If there was an opening in the forest, how come the satellite had never detected people moving into or through it? Living and working under the triple-canopy jungle would be hell for an agrarian society like the Vietnamese. He knew enough about their culture from the prebriefing to know they would try to plant gardens anywhere the could find a patch of sunlight. Their diet depended on fresh vegetables, year round. Before he could get to the clearing, he had the answer, as something stabbed him below the knee and slashed his forearm. He stepped back and saw a barbed wire fence.

He cursed himself for not watching where he was going, for daydreaming about the clearing. What if the fence had been booby trapped? Or worse, if he had set off silent alarms? With Zavello on the ground, how would he explain ruining the mission before it began?

He stepped back and a whispered a warning to Greiner,

who had adopted the habit of clicking his teeth twice to answer in the affirmative.

Swayne checked closely for trip wires. He found nothing but barbed wire, overgrown by vines and grasses. Even though he and Greiner had not walked out of the forest yet, the fence apparently encircled the clearing and extended into the forest as far as any shaft of daylight—or satellite view—could reach at any time of the year.

He made a mental note to get close-up, daytime satellite pictures of the area, including topographic studies. He wanted to know what areas were flat and where any natural obstacles like streams or marshes would be found. Later, when it came time to call in the extraction helicopters to lift out prisoners, he would know where to put them. By then, he would have finished his recon. He would know how many prisoners were to go, thus how many helicopters were needed for them, their Delta Force rescuers, and the Spartans.

Listen to me, he cautioned. He had not proven yet that there were any prisoners. And if there were, that they were Caucasian. More specifically, American. It could very well be a political prison for former members of the South Vietnamese government, or former ARVN officers. Or just a lot of poor thieves and murderers, common criminals the Communists would never acknowledge having in their perfect society.

That was for later. He detoured deeper into the jungle to avoid the thicker undergrowth and began walking in an arc, following the fence to its side closest to the camp. Finally, not five minutes before the dawn's early light would betray them, he found a spot where he could watch through the camp's wire. He decided against climbing a tree like Night Runner. He hadn't done that kind of thing since he was a kid, anyhow. Night Runner was far more capable of camouflaging himself; he had already proven that on the march earlier. The last thing Swayne wanted was to appear as a cancer on the trunk of a tree, visible to guards who had spent their waking lives standing watch for endless hours looking out into the woods. By now they must know every tree in the forest like family.

Rather than choosing his spot, the spot chose him. He and Greiner had to creep in to the edge of the undergrowth less than a hundred meters from the first wire obstacle. It gave them a good field of view, at least to the outer buildings of the camp. He could get no closer, because somebody had made a half-hearted effort to clear the undergrowth. He could get no farther away, because just two steps backward obscured the camp altogether. So he and Greiner found a thick spot and lay on their bellies, watching between finger-sized saplings, keeping their heads near the ground. He looked back over his shoulder toward the clearing. In the gloom of first dawn, he could see just a glimpse of the hills they had left behind, where Zavello and his prisoner would spend their day. The clouds had lowered, obscuring both peaks and the saddle, so the entire range of hills looked like a flat-topped mesa. He turned off the night vision goggles and switched his binoculars from night to daytime function.

As if he had just switched on the NITA effect instead of turning off the night devices, the day came alive.

Moc Ly Labor Camp, Vietnam
0627 Hours Local

SWAYNE'S HEART HAMMERED at the latest curse from Zavello. Greiner, lying on his belly so he could watch the rear and flanks, flinched so hard he kicked his captain's boot sole and murmured an apology.

Swayne didn't care about that. He kept listening for Zavello to follow up. The old man might not be aware of it, but he was transmitting the sound of heavy breathing. Veterans of the field kept the microphone at the corners of their mouths so they could give it a sideways kiss, yet keep it out of the way of exhaling, either from the nose or mouth. Puffs of air would pop the microphone and hurt the ears of any-body plugged in.

When Swayne could still hear breathing and the smacking of lips, he surmised that Zavello was still conscious. So he had not been overcome by his prisoner or an attacker, after all. He might have dropped his rifle or gotten a cramp in his leg. Swayne could see that the previous night's march had taken a lot out of the colonel. In one sense, he felt sorry for him. In another, he was glad. It meant the colonel would never butt in on an operational team again.

NIGHT RUNNER BARELY gave Zavello a thought. "One, this is Two, can you see what's going on inside the wire?" He kept his voice low, so he wouldn't give away his exposed position in the tree.

"Negative activity. The buildings must be blocking our view."

"Check your video feed."

SWAYNE TURNED ON the night vision binoculars, leaving the caps on the lenses, so the visual image would not interfere with the video play. What he saw made his hands tremble. Caucasian men. In their fifties. An entire file of them in close-up, only heads and shoulders visible. He could tell by the auburn, gray, and blond hair, especially the full beards on some of them, that they were mostly Caucasians, except for two African-Americans. He wanted to stare, trying to pick out some feature, some expression, something that would help him identify his father. He dared not let his emotions run away with him.

"Zoom out," he said. "Give me a view of the camp lay-out." What he saw frightened him. As the camera lens pulled back, he could tell the men had their hands tied behind them. He could see their armed guards, serious looks on all the faces as they escorted them toward a parade ground at the center of the camp.

He saw posts in the ground and a formation of soldiers, perhaps seventy-five or eighty, meaning the camp was guarded by a company of soldiers, with many more certainly on duty patrolling the wire and standing sentry in the towers.

"That's as wide a shot as I can get," Night Runner said. "I'll pan to give you the full layout."

Swayne memorized the details as they swept by in slow motion. Several things struck him at once. He counted twenty-six prisoners coming from three buildings. On the outside of each of the barracks-type dwellings stood a group of women and children. Beyond that, there were only five other buildings. One was clearly an administration building, and another looked to be a chow hall. A smaller facility was a shower facility and head. An even smaller shack, fenced in and reinforced with coils of concertina, seemed to be the only cell block in the place. That left only one building for the camp's garrison.

Swayne figured that a building that size would hold maybe a platoon of soldiers in the security detachment, twenty-five men comfortably, forty cramped and double-bunked.

"Show me a close-up of the towers," he ordered.

The picture shot an alarming dose of adrenaline into Swayne's bloodstream. Each tower had three men inside, all looking outward. The main tower at the entrance gate held four men. Night Runner panned to the base of that tower, where Swayne could see two men at each of the pair of sally ports.

This meant trouble. There would be no reason to keep such a large force here. The barracks and mess would not support the hundred soldiers in formation. The camp commander had brought in reinforcements.

The knowledge set hairs tingling all over Swayne's body. He tried to calm himself. Likely, the prisoners were in no danger. Somebody—they probably didn't even know who—

had struck a missile and its carrier truck just a few miles from here, in the heart of the central highlands. It had made the People's Republic nervous. They had sent troops to guard all their military treasures and terrible secrets. The country was on a high state of alert, no more than that.

He felt sad at a second realization. The fighting force of one hundred here would scrap any Delta Force rescue mission. The numbers of helicopters needed to land the troops and rescue prisoners would be far too large an armada. Too hard to maintain surprise, even with stealth helicopters. A couple of phone calls—even the Vietnamese peasants might have cell phones—and a countrywide alert would go out. The enemy would be waiting, and even the best forces would have difficulty getting through the wire. The jungle canopy would prevent ordinary rappelling or roping down. Any large firefight would be sure to kill many of the prisoners in those buildings and the civilians. One armor-piercing round would go through every shack in the compound, killing men and women alike.

The civilians. "Let me take a close look at the women and children," he said. Night Runner's lens found them after a second's delay. The women were Vietnamese, and the children were either Asian-Caucasian or Afro-Asians. Those were families of the prisoners.

Swayne shook his head. Some of the kids were in their teens, some were infants.

Before he could reflect, two curse words, the same word from both Zavello and Friel, upset any hope that the Force Recon team would be able to remain hidden in position, watching and waiting until the alert status had been diminished, until the reinforced garrison went back to its normal size.

Swayne looked up from his binoculars as Zavello's obscenity was cut off in midword. This time the sounds that came through his open microphone included the deep moan of an injured man. And to Swayne's horror, the growling of a huge cat, like the opening of a Warner Brothers movie.

Friel's curse came with a dizzying sweep of Night Runner's video lens as Swayne put his eyes to the binoculars again. A pair of guards each had pinned three of the men against a setup that looked like an oversized hitching post out of the Western movies. The crossbar hit their backs just below their shoulder blades. Their bound hands were thrown over the bar, and then their wrists were pulled against their backs by a rope tied around their waists.

"We going to let them execute those poor bastards?"

"Shut up, Henry." Swayne and Night Runner said it at the same time.

Swayne could tell that Night Runner had become as excited as he was. Neither of them had expected anything like this. On cue, a voice came at them from the Operational Mission Control Center.

"Eagle One, this is Eagle base, over."

Swayne gave Zavello a chance to respond, hoping that he would, knowing he would not. The microphone had gone silent—what was it?—several minutes ago?

"Eagle base, this is Spartan One, Eagle One is out of action."

"Captain Swayne?" The voice betrayed panic. "What happened to him? We didn't hear anything over the net."

You were listening, Swayne thought. *You know something happened.* More likely, they wanted to be told that nothing had happened, but he said, "The eagle is down. There's no way to tell why." Swayne gave the OMCC confirmation of the GPS coordinates that he had already transmitted twice, both last night and this morning. "We left him behind to guard our prisoner while we pulled off the recon."

"You left him behind?"

Swayne resented the note of accusation in the voice. Somebody was looking for a place to point a finger in case Zavello's death might need an explanation or justification. Swayne didn't take the bait. Every bit as important as what

might have happened to the colonel was what seemed about
to happen inside the camp.

"Are you getting the video feed from here?" Swayne
wanted to know.

"Negative—affirmative—stand by."

The man left his mike open, and Swayne could hear mur-
muring coming muffled from the background. He was holding his hand over the mike, trying to deal with the
information that somebody else was giving him about the
pictures.

Finally, the voice came back. "Uh, roger. Turn the screen
so I can see it. There. No. Now leave alone. Roger, I see the
pictures. What the hell is going on?"

"They're setting up for a firing squad," Swayne said dryly.
A rank of six men had lined up no more than twenty meters
from the three prisoners. Each carried an AK-47. Each stood
in a rigid position, arrayed like a plastic soldier, rifle held
across his chest at port arms.

The voice on the radio rose two octaves. "They're setting
up for a firing squad. Spartan One, report your intentions."

Great. The guy was going to pieces. Three men about to
die, and the best this desk commando could do was give
Swayne back his own words. And demand a report that
would put Swayne on record in case the guy needed to cover
his butt.

"Stand by," Swayne said. To get the bonehead out of his
ears so he could think. Usually he had to sort things out with
bullets flying, mind-numbing noise, men howling, attackers
attacking. Not this time. Now, all was silent. He should be
able to get on top of this.

But he couldn't. His nerves felt every bit as raw as when
the bullets sang by his ears. The clock was running out on
the victims of that firing squad. He saw a squad marching in
file, flanking the execution site. Too near the surface of his
mind, he heard the grating voice of his grandfather: *Whatcha
gonna do now, boy?* The senior senator from South Carolina,

always ready to rise again, always handy to repeat his doubts that Swayne didn't belong in uniform.

A Vietnamese soldier went to each of the condemned in turn to tie a black blindfold over his eyes. *Think, Jack, think!*

What was really happening here? Okay, a firing squad, but why?

Punishment? A court-martial penalty, perhaps, for an escape attempt? That didn't make sense. That was not worth death. Even if it was, why assemble a company from outside the garrison?

Retaliation for the strike against the missiles? That made even less sense. The prisoners would have had nothing to do with that, and none of the Vietnamese would even suspect it. They would not be sending a message to America, because, for all intents, America did not know the prisoners existed. Unless this was going to be a videotaped, public execution, there was no point in it. Besides, the Vietnamese, if they were going to retaliate, would have to say what they were retaliating for.

Swayne's heart pounded against his sternum. He pushed himself up on his elbows, so it would not hammer against the ground as well. What if one of those three men were his father? Could he lie here and let it happen? All these years thinking he was dead. Then considering the possibility that he was alive. Now, of all things, witnessing his father's death? What surreal nonsense was that?

Swayne saw the rifles rise and heard Night Runner clearing his throat. *Were they going to watch these three men die?* Night Runner wanted to know.

Swayne heard another soft curse. He recognized it as the voice of the man in the OMCC. "Spartan, this is Eagle, stand by for orders. Repeat, do not take action at this time. Acknowledge."

There it was. The order from somebody who did not fully understand what was going on, thus had ordered a course of inaction, rather than action. Better to do nothing then do the wrong thing. Swayne had seen that reasoning before. The order had come from a senior officer. Even if the man was wrong, Swayne had no business doing anything but obeying.

One of the Vietnamese, a noncom or officer, standing at the flank of the firing squad, raised his right arm with the red, blue, and gold national flag.

Swayne understood. Everything that he ever thought about himself and his place in the Marine Corps, as well as his relationship to his father, had come down to this instant. He understood what the Vietnamese were up to, even if he could not guess why. He knew what he must do.

"Runner, Friel, take out the firing squad and as many soldiers as you can. Then get the hell out."

"Belay that," the voice from the OMCC ordered. "Do not fire. Do not fire."

He got his answer in the form of the string of rifle shots and the sounds of 20 mm rounds spitting from Friel's Blowpipe gun. Each spitting sound was followed by the noise of a huge Velcro strip being ripped apart as the round's rocket propulsion system kicked in.

With each rip of the air, the 20 mm missile launcher fired a high explosive round set to proximity fuse. Like an artillery shell, it blew up just short of the target, piercing some soldiers through with shrapnel, killing others with concussion.

FRIEL BY GOD knew that the captain would do the right thing. As usual, he waited until the last freaking tick, but at least he did it. One of these days the son of a bitch was going to stall his officer ass too long and leave some Marine with a tit in the wringer.

He and the chief fired at the same time without a word of coordination. Because Friel was in the crotch of the tree to Night Runner's right, he would take the three shooters to the right. He had already set up his ammunition, selecting area fire. A radar return to the tip of the round would tell it when it was ten meters from a solid target. That was the cue to explode, sending shrapnel in an expanding funnel ahead of the explosion, peppering a target with concussion, noise, and irregular pieces of hard steel.

By the time he had launched the first round, Friel saw the first shooter on the left, Night Runner's man, drop, clutching at his pelvis. Low. Piss-poor shooting from the chief. But Friel didn't have time to criticize the shot, or even watch the flight of his own round. He had swung to the formation of soldiers, touching off three more of the deadly rounds. Even those he could not watch all the way to their destination. By the time the first round had struck, he was drawing a bead on the nearest guard tower. Once that round was off, he swung to the second. Then, across a compound in the distance, not far from Swayne, he could see the top of the main tower. He popped one more round in that direction.

"Henry, come on," Night Runner yelled to him. Friel stepped backward. He did not want to jump the ten feet. Hard impacts, even running hard, still hurt his newly healed jaw, broken in four places on that last mission. Night Runner caught his heel and helped lower him to the ground.

"Thanks, Gunny."

But Night Runner was not waiting for thanks or giving your-welcomes. Friel dashed after him into the forest. Stealth was no longer a factor. They needed to put a forest of trees between themselves and the camp before things got hot.

Almost a full minute elapsed before the first round was fired in their direction. By that time, it would have taken armor-piercing cannon shot to reach into the woods. Still, Friel ducked involuntarily at the explosions behind them. The gooks had mortars?

SWAYNE WATCHED THE chaos unfold. After the first explosions, everybody in the Vietnamese formation not blown down either threw themselves on the ground or ran for cover behind the flimsy buildings. Another force of perhaps fifty soldiers broke from two of the billeting areas, a reaction force adding to the confusion by mixing with soldiers already in the open. It took a while for their officers to sort and regroup their men into units. Some soldiers charged at the wire and fired through it. Some rounds set off frag grenades and flares inside the security wire, and at least two men shooting into the ground detonated mines. In all, the picture was that of an ant-hill disturbed by poking at it with a stick. A detachment of soldiers herded prisoners and their families back into a barracks. Taking the condemned out of harm's way. Swayne factored that into his assessment of the bizarre situation.

"Spartan Two, this is Spartan One, what are your presets?" Swayne asked, wanting to know the frequencies Night Runner had set on the concussion grenades, the boomers that could be detonated by remote control.

"Shit," Friel said, and Swayne knew that he had forgotten to drop grenades.

"Charlie-two," Night Runner said.

Swayne wished they had brought one of their remote-controlled ambush kits. As green as those troops were inside the prison camp, he could have kept them pinned down until nightfall.

He could not very well see what was going on, but he heard enough screaming and shouting to understand that the officers and noncoms were not having an easy time getting their men together.

The voice from the OMCC still shouted at him, demanding a response. Like most men who panicked under fire, he didn't stop talking long enough to listen.

No matter. Swayne's field radio had an override feature that allowed the soldier in the field to suppress transmissions from headquarters. He used it. "Eagle, this is Spartan One, stop shouting. Right now."

The officer, offended, had to put himself on record—for all radio conversations and video were recorded: "I gave you an order not to fire. You be aware, Captain, that this is grounds for court-martial."

He went on, but Swayne cut him off again. "I'm going on record here. Stop interfering with a team in the middle of a firefight."

The shouting stopped. Swayne said, "We can debate the order later. Your ass is covered, and I can take the heat. For now, stay off the radio so we can exfiltrate the hot zone. Your hysteria makes it difficult for us to communicate. Full report to follow."

Swayne never thought he would see the day when he wished that Zavello was on the radio back at the OMCC instead of the officer, a senior in rank but a rookie in experience, who had made his ear weary.

Zavello. He needed to get in touch with his boss. But there were other things to tend to first. Most urgent was the sound of trucks coming down the road from the Ho Chi Minh Trail toward the prison camp. Lots of trucks, from what he could hear.

The Vietnamese must have another company, even an entire battalion, standing off, ready to react to this camp?

So. The Vietnamese had set a trap for him and the team, perhaps expecting them to try to sneak in but certainly knowing that they would be coming. Very possibly they had set up the firing squad as a ruse, in the hope that Americans would react to it, perhaps attempt a rescue of prisoners. Whether the executions were real or staged did not matter now. The Spartans had reacted. For the time being, the real executions had been prevented. Real or faked, the team had transmitted video. Politicians and diplomats could see Americans if they needed proof. Not that it mattered now. None of them would get out of Vietnam alive. The thought struck him at his core. If his father was in that camp, Swayne would never see him, never know him. He tried to reconcile that notion with himself. No way. He would have to deal with it later. For now, he was responsible for the survival of Greiner and the rest of his team.

He put himself into the mind of his enemy. What would

he do in the position of the commander now under attack?

First, he would secure the camp and the precious American prisoners, using most or all of the troops already inside the wire. Second, he would deploy the reaction force in two elements, one to hit at the spot where Night Runner and Friel had opened the attack. He would order the second element to sweep the woods for at least a hundred meters around the camp perimeter to clear out any other enemy pockets and try to catch a retreating force.

"We have to move," he said to Greiner. "Quickly." Swayne used two camouflaged strips of bad-ass duct tape to secure a pair of grenades, one on each of two trees about six feet apart, on the side toward the camp. Between the two grenades, he ran a trip wire at knee level.

The shooting from inside the camp had stopped. He could see a small force forming inside the gate, but nobody had made a move to come out yet. He decided that they were probably waiting for the reaction force. They would either lead the force to Night Runner's ambush site, or else they would point it out and stay inside the wire. Since they were acting so hesitant, probably the latter.

Swayne told Greiner to begin backtracking to the first device they had planted. "Find the first booby trap and wait for me before we arm it."

By now, the ground had begun to tremble with the rumble of approaching trucks. Swayne could tell that the excitement level had dropped inside the wire. Since no more shots had come from the jungle, the soldiers felt safe. He knew the thinking of green troops. They wanted the attack to be no more than a hit-and-run contact. Some were lighting cigarettes. Some were leaning against buildings, like soldiers all over the world, laughing at their own terror, trying to hide the horror of the killings of their own men beneath a covering of black humor. By now, they might even have found a way to congratulate themselves. They had prevented the enemy from getting inside the camp. Even though they had lost perhaps more than a dozen men, they were considering it a victory. Swayne smirked. He had seen the same kind of reasoning applied to many a disaster, even among American armed forces.

The trucks rolled into sight.

Swayne could not believe his own agitation. The nearest soldier was perhaps two hundred yards away, so he had plenty of time to do what he needed to and escape. But that single, haunting thought had returned. Escape would mean running from the camp where his father was held captive. How could he do that? How would he ever know, if he ran away?

Then, of course, it occurred him. How would he know if he stayed? Other than becoming an inmate himself, he could not. So, as the first truck pulled up, Swayne laid out two thirty-round magazines for his M-16. Like the one already in his rifle, they were taped bottom to bottom, so he could eject one, flip it over, reinsert it, and begin firing immediately.

The first magazine he emptied into the wire among the soldiers standing at the base of the smoldering watch tower. The second, he fired into the canvas of the first truck. By the time he had ejected and loaded a third, the first rounds had smacked into the trees above him. The forest protected him but also gave him only a few narrow lanes of fire. Into each one where he saw another truck in the convoy of six, he shot a short burst. Then he turned to run. Something hit him in the back and threw him to the ground. It was as if somebody had whacked him with a shovel on the back of his left shoulder.

"Captain, you all right?"

Greiner. Swayne realized he must have cried out.

"One this is Two?" *Runner. Concerned?*

"I'm nine-by," Swayne said, trying not to strain the words between his teeth, hoping to put both of them at ease.

He struggled to his feet, his left arm useless, as if it had gone to sleep. His fingers tingled. He couldn't make them hold onto the forestock of his rifle. Far above his head, slugs snapped into the foliage, trimming leaves and small branches, sending them flying like salad out of a Veg-O-Matic without the lid. Swayne got to his feet and began running, his arm flopping at his side. He checked the front of his shoulder opposite the pain at his back. No exit wound. That meant the round had probably hit something—a branch or even the ground—before striking him. It had been tumbling when it struck, possibly causing more damage than an untouched round piercing his shoulder through. He just hoped it had lost most of its momentum before striking him.

As in most of their missions, the Force Recon Marines did not wear body armor; too heavy.

As Swayne plowed his way through the foliage, he was glad for the opportunity to run. Sneaking around all the time could wear a man out. Nothing like getting shot to elevate the pulse.

"I hear footsteps," Greiner said. "Maybe five meters."

Swayne reacted to the tentative tone in Greiner's voice, not wanting to alarm him. Or worse, to have him start shooting blindly at a noise. "It's me, with nobody behind."

He saw Greiner on one knee, his rifle muzzle swinging away from him as he burst through the brush. Greiner kept his rifle trained down Swayne's back trail, even as he pointed with his left hand to the grenade left behind this morning.

Swayne bent over the grenade and opened its control panel. He had already made the sets, and now he activated the timing device, set for thirty seconds, and the detonation mode, set for motion. He scooped out a depression in the packed, dead leaves, set the grenade into it, and covered it over. He was glad to find that he could wiggle the fingers of his left hand. His wrist worked, and he could bend the arm at the elbow. So far, he didn't feel any wetness soaking down his arm.

"Check out the back of my left shoulder," he said.

"Jeez, sir, you've been shot."

Even with the pain, Swayne could not suppress a guffaw. "I'm fine," he said, trying to make a recovery of embarrassing the kid. "How's the bleeding? Anything arterial?"

"No squirting." Greiner pulled the strap of his pack away from the shoulder. "Your pack strap is almost all the way cut through. The blood looks like no more than a shot glass. If you don't have any broken bones—"

"Minor. We'll deal with it later." Swayne stood up and shucked himself back into the pack. The numbness had left his arm, except for the wound itself, which had began to sting, as if he had fallen on pavement and scraped himself raw.

He saw that his brusqueness had wounded the kid. He felt ashamed, because Greiner had only shown his concern for him. He could not know what was going through Swayne's mind. A minor wound was the least of his problems.

"I'll lead out. You watch our six."

"Yes, sir," Greiner said.

"Let me know if the bleeding gets any worse."

"Yes, sir."

Behind them, the firing began to escalate from a simple firefight to a small war. Swayne, still troubled about running away from the camp, could not help feeling some satisfaction. He had read about American soldiers landing for the first time in Vietnam. Until they got some experience under their belts, they were prone to wasting ammunition shooting everywhere against the more combat-experienced Vietcong. Now the tables had been reversed. Almost nobody on the ground back there had any combat experience, of that he was sure. The greater their volume of fire, the less likely that any of them would know that they were not receiving return fire. Swayne knew that, until the firing stopped, nobody would be coming out into the forest after them. All that reckless shooting made it too dangerous to be walking around in the woods.

He settled into a comfortable pace, faster than walking, slower than jogging. No point in crashing through the forest. Yet, there was no reason to be quiet, either. All he wanted to do now was to put some distance between himself and the camp. He wouldn't even worry about hiding their trail until he met up with Night Runner. Then he'd let the warrior worry about that.

In the distance, he could hear the racket of gunfire becoming more sporadic, like microwave popcorn nearly done.

He kept up the quick walk. He deduced from the noise that officers had gotten control of their panicked men. Swayne knew he had drawn a lot of blood. For green troops, a huge shock.

Now the officers and noncoms would have their work cut out for them. They had to reorganize with the survivors and prepare them to attack both positions that the Force Recon Marines had used to make their strikes.

Swayne found the next spot where he had left a grenade earlier that morning. He checked the trip wire, opened the casing of the device, and started the activation timer. He checked his GPS and signaled Greiner as he stepped out in the direction of the staging area where they had left Zavello and their prisoner.

Zavello. He had given the colonel barely more than a thought since the man had signed off earlier today. Now he felt a new sense of urgency. Rather than worry about the fantasy of his father being inside that camp, he should devote his full concern to Zavello's well-being. Let the booby traps handle the Vietnamese.

The grenades nearest the camp, both attached to trees, would be set off by the trip wire. Somebody going through the position where Swayne had fired and left the brass would follow the trail. Once troops behind him saw that it was safe, they would rush toward the tree. Thirty seconds after the wire snapped, the grenade would go off. Anybody in front of the tree would be struck by shrapnel. Very likely, each grenade's explosive blast would snap off the tree trunk, dropping the eighty-foot monsters on any troops beneath its arc.

The second grenade had been set with a motion-detection trigger activated thirty seconds after Swayne set the timer. Somebody walking over the ground would either kick it or step on it, setting it off two seconds later.

This last one was connected to a wire at head level. Nervous already, the soldiers would be looking at the ground for trip wires and disturbed leaves. With their eyes down, their heads would brush the wire, pulling the grenade from its nest in the crook of a limb. It would go off about four feet above a man's head. After that, any troops on their trail would be so careful they could not gain any ground on the Force Recon team.

But it was that first set of explosions, the tree-felling grenades, that Swayne listened for.

When they came, Swayne was surprised at how well the forest muffled the sound. If they hadn't slowed down, he might not have heard it at all above the noise they were making on the march. He did hear the crackling of yet another firefight, as panicked soldiers reacted.

He knelt on one knee and fumbled with his remote transmitter, extending the antenna. He dropped it once and cursed. The left arm wasn't working as well as he had thought, after all.

"Check my shoulder," he told Greiner.

"Already done, sir. It's still bleeding, but nothing life-threatening. You don't feel dizzy?"

"Negative."

"Sir, you want to take a minute for first aid, some gauze and a bandage?"

"Negative." Swayne worked the menu buttons, finding the frequency that Night Runner had programmed into the grenades he had left at his first ambush site. Once he dialed the settings, he didn't hesitate. There might be no soldiers at that spot, or there could be an entire platoon gathered. It didn't matter. What was important was to add to the confusion. He touched both detonator buttons at once, surprised at how weak his left thumb had gotten from the injury to his shoulder.

Night Runner's boomers cracked the heavens. The noise, coming to him directly across the open, grassy area, was not filtered by so many trees as his own explosion. The white light, visible even by day, the blast, the concussion, and for anybody nearby, the shrapnel. All that would make any unit nervous. A group without combat experience would be terrified. The officers and noncoms would have their hands full, trying to get that group to go into the forest any deeper. Even if they were capable of pulling it off, any soldiers who ran into the next set of booby traps would dig in and risk courts-martial over the certainty of death that the Marines had left behind them.

Good officers would find a way around the problems that the Marines had created, literally. They would pull back their men and reorganize, conducting a large sweep, possibly two sweeps around the open area. That way they would avoid following the trail of explosive bread crumbs that their enemy had left behind.

That wouldn't matter to the Spartans, except that such a maneuver would take time to organize and execute. Their job now would be to pick up Zavello and the prisoner. They would find another area suitable for a landing zone, an area far from the prison camp. They would call in an extraction bird. End of story.

Within a day or two, the Americans—Swayne had began to think of them as Americans now—would be removed from the camp, relocated to other sites within Vietnam. Nobody outside Vietnam would ever know about the situation, except in the video that had been transmitted already to higher headquarters. It wasn't enough to matter. Swayne knew that from his previous experiences. Once, he had delivered a videotape of mass murder being committed inside Kosovo. He knew that the video had gone straight to the top of the administration. Nothing had happened. Absolutely nothing. In fact, the tapes had been ordered destroyed so that nothing *could* happen. Nobody wanted to handle such a volatile situation in the open.

This would be another political stalemate. If the Americans said anything about prisoners, the Vietnamese would claim the entire scene had been staged by a Hollywood production crew. If the Vietnamese accused the Americans of invading their country, the Americans could produce satellite images and ground video of strategic missiles exploding inside Vietnam. A Mexican standoff, Vietnam style.

As they began marching toward the rally point where they would meet up with Night Runner and Friel, Swayne felt that he had left something of himself back there at the camp, not including some of his blood from the wound. He did feel weak and dizzy. Not only physically but also emotionally. What if his father was back there? Perhaps he would know that the attack had been a rescue attempt, after all these years. Of course, he would have no idea that his own son would be involved. Whatever he thought, all hopes of freedom would be dashed by now.

For all Swayne knew, military officers on the scene had lined up the entire inmate population and shot them down in retaliation for the deaths suffered by the Vietnamese, taking the initiative out of the hands of politicians and diplomats. He had helped kill his own—

Nonsense. His old man wasn't inside that camp. He was dead. Killed in action. Later listed as missing in action. Dead then, or dead now. Dead in any case. Instead of putting his wits to work on a fantasy that could never be realized, he should be focusing on Zavello, whom they hadn't heard from in—he looked at his watch—more than twenty minutes.

Where the hell is Zavello?

"Sir?" Greiner asked.

"Nothing," Swayne said, coming off as far too hostile to the kid. He hadn't realized he had even spoken his thoughts aloud.

As he and Greiner approached the rally point, Swayne exchanged the sign and countersign with Night Runner.

"Spartan One and Four coming in."

"This is Two, roger. Washington."

"Denzel."

The exchange was a formality, really. Only somebody who had access to the discrete radio frequencies, including the unique scramblers invented for those radios and compatible with the satellite transmitters, could have used the sets. Besides, each of the team members knew each other, so that even if an enemy had stolen a radio, he could not mimic their voices. Still, they kept to the procedure.

The rally point was not a safe place to stay, let alone trade thoughts. Neither team knew whether the other had been followed. So they set off for a secondary rally point at once, Friel taking the lead, Night Runner taking the tail so he could watch behind and cover their tracks.

In an hour, they had put the camp far enough behind them that even if there had been shooting going on, the team could not have heard it.

While Friel and Greiner found positions to provide security, Night Runner and Swayne put their heads together. The priority now was to locate Zavello. Swayne had tried calling several times. With less sophisticated radios, a Force Recon Marine in the field might worry about terrain or vegetation blocking the radio signal. Not with the satellite overhead. Since Zavello had not answered, they could only assume that something happened to him. What's more, they knew that if an enemy had taken the colonel, one of their radios was in the hands of the bad guys. So the first thing they did was shut off their mikes to discuss the situation and a plan to remedy it.

"What you think?" Swayne asked. "The prisoner got to him?"

Night Runner wagged his head. "Don't know. When we

left, the little guy was tied up. I don't know the colonel. Would he do something stupid?"

"You mean release the guy's hands so he could take a leak or something? You wouldn't think that a combat veteran would make such a rookie mistake," Swayne said. "But I don't know him in the field. If somebody were to call him on the radio and ask him whether to untie a prisoner's hands so he could take—"

"He'd say, 'Let him piss his pants.' "

They exchanged worried looks. Night Runner raised one eyebrow in the form of a question.

Swayne shook his head in disgust. He wondered if the little glitches had as much to do with unraveling large-scale missions as they did with the small ones. For the lack of a fresh battery in a GPS system in Afghanistan, a Delta Force operator had transmitted incorrect coordinates, bringing bombs in on a friendly position.

More than one lost armored convoy had traveled in a circle at night and attacked its own tail end. They both knew of such instances.

"Nothing to do but go up there and see for ourselves," Swayne said.

"We'll probably find the two of them asleep. The old man probably shut off his radio so he wouldn't be disturbed." The worry in Night Runner's eyes betrayed his lack of belief in that scenario.

Swayne was not willing to take chances, either. He brought everybody together and briefed them on a tactical approach to the staging area where they had left Zavello and the prisoner. He directed everybody to the team's internal alternate radio frequency. Before changing his own radio's setting, he notified the OMCC that it would not be a standard frequency that Zavello would know. He would have to call the command center, authenticate his transmission, and get the new frequency before he could talk to the team. If he did suddenly come up and try to contact the Spartans, Swayne directed, the OMCC should not reveal any information on their location or intentions.

"It's possible that Eagle One may have lost his radio to the enemy. Don't take any chances," he told the officer in command at the OMCC. The man's reply was abrupt. The tone of it told Swayne that he would call him on the carpet in the debriefing of this mission. For him, this wasn't about Zavello. This was a power issue. Swayne felt a twinge of the same disgust that Friel voiced about officers, staff officers in particular.

NIGHT RUNNER TOOK the team on a route that angled away from the staging area and hooked around the hill farthest away from the saddle. He came at the position from well beyond the labor camp. That way gave the best chance of surprising anybody waiting in ambush for them to return from the firefight. Any Vietnamese scouting party that knew about today's strike at the camp would focus in that direction.

He crossed the trail that the team, Zavello, and the Vietnamese prisoner had made going into the staging area the previous night. He didn't have to look for signs. He simply referred to yesterday's track on the GPS, which would not be erased until after the debriefing, and then only after being downloaded into a computer archive. He stopped long enough to be sure of two things: first, that they had not been followed into the staging area last night; second, that nobody had taken Zavello or the others out along this path. He couldn't find any tracks that didn't belong.

Night Runner took the team within fifty meters of the staging area, holding below it on the river side. After Swayne put out security, he huddled with his captain. They left their radio microphones on so Greiner and Friel would know what was up.

Swayne nodded, wanting Night Runner to brief him.

"The breeze is coming off the top," Night Runner said.

"So that's why you're wrinkling your nose," Swayne said. "What is it? Smoke? Zavello wouldn't light a—"

"It's not smoke. It's blood. I smell blood."

"What else? I heard it in your voice. There's something else."

"That tiger."

Friel cursed under his breath but into his open mike. The bushes on either side of the perimeter rustled, as both junior Spartans checked around themselves. Afraid, Swayne thought wryly, that they had knelt down too near the animal lying in wait.

"So, what do you recommend?" Swayne asked.

Night Runner directed the team to hold in place for five minutes, as he made a detour toward the staging area and got ahead of them. He said he would move in on the position from the right flank of the Force Recon team, as they worked their way uphill. He didn't say so, but he expected that the three white men would make the most noise, and he would be in position to see if anybody—or any animal—reacted to the sound.

"I also recommend that you have Greiner patch up that shoulder before you move out," Night Runner said.

Swayne smiled. "Wouldn't want the smell of blood to attract any uninvited company."

Friel cursed again. "That ain't funny. I saw *Jaws*, you know."

As he walked clear of the perimeter, Night Runner caught the eye of Friel. The kid from Boston gave him a thumbs-up, a wink, and a nod.

"I want you to know that I'm going to blame you if I wake up in the kitty litter," Friel said, setting up security as Greiner prepared to work on Swayne's wound.

Night Runner backtracked a short distance before going uphill so he would not have to be in the line of fire of his team if anything broke loose. Once he got to within thirty meters of the position, he began gliding rather than walking, taking a full five seconds for every step. It still was not quiet enough for him. Not as quiet as the Montagnard had been that night in the dark, when he had stepped around the bamboo viper. After he heard the team begin moving below him, he cut himself a little slack. He could dare to walk a little faster because of the racket the others made. Still, even moving slowly, he reached the edge of the staging area first.

While the team was still about twenty meters away, he murmured into his microphones, "Hold what you've got."

He went through his senses, one by one. He let each one give him its report. Because the worst of it was what he could see, he closed his eyes and ran through the inventory again.

"All clear," he reported, opening his eyes. He stepped into the pocket of the forest where they had spent last night together. The fragile undergrowth had been pushed down when the team left before dark that morning. But by now it had been thrashed by activity. He searched for clues, waiting for the others to come.

Friel walked into the position first, and saw first what Night Runner expected anybody who relied only on his eyes to see: the Vietnamese sentry.

"Shit's sake," Friel said, swiping his hand in front of his face to clear away the smell and the swarming flies. "Where's his head?"

"Where's the colonel?" Swayne asked as he joined the others. He turned to Greiner, who had joined up with Friel to stare at the sight beneath their feet. The Vietnamese prisoner, his hands still bound together, his fingers still taped, lay on his belly, his feet uphill. Below him, a splash of blood ran for about two meters. He had bled out in a gush.

"Freaking tiger took his head off in one bite?" Friel asked.

Swayne was as stunned as anyone else on the team, but he gathered his wits at once. "Scouts out," he ordered. The Marines knew at once that they should not have had to be told. They moved into the forest a few meters. Swayne saw that they had not gone as far as they usually would. Both of them had kept clear of the downwind smell of the gore.

Swayne didn't blame them. He moved out of the breeze and waited for Night Runner to make a circuit of the area. When he came back, it was clear he had found something. Clearly, it was not good news.

"The colonel?" Swayne asked.

Night Runner shook his head, then realized it might be misinterpreted. "He's been taken away. Carried off."

"Man, get me out of this place," Friel said. "If I ever leave this goddamned Vietnam, I'm never coming back again."

"Henry, stow it," Swayne said. He turned to Night Runner. "Carried off? By the tiger?"

"Negative. He's alive, as far as I can tell." Night Runner had given his report over the radio so that the team and the staff in the OMCC could get a grip on the situation. Now he signaled with the snipping motion. They both shut off their mikes.

"I found the Vietnamese soldier's head down the slope a ways. Definitely the tiger."

Swayne nodded. He had seen the paw print in the soft ground beneath the wash of blood. It looked nearly as big around as a Frisbee.

"I don't get it," he said. "If the tiger didn't carry him off, then who? What?"

In answer, Night Runner took him to the edge of the area where the scuffle had taken place. He pushed away the foliage. In the shadows lay a brown piece of cardboard from a ration packet. Splashes of blood formed a pattern over the words, Meal Vegetarian, Pasta with Sauce. At first glance it looked to be a partial paw print of the tiger. Then the regular, rounded parts of the image fell into place as a unified picture. A partial footprint. A man's footprint. A man who walked about the forest in bare feet.

ZAVELLO OPENED HIS eye and said to his captors, "I suppose you're all wondering why I called you all together." The very effort of speaking sent streaks of white-hot pain shooting through his head as his words ran the gauntlet of his thick tongue, conical teeth, and tingling lips. He knew he had a concussion, at least, maybe something worse. A stroke or something. Hell, he had grown old enough and had high enough blood pressure for a stroke without being bashed on the side of the head with a rifle butt.

Neither of the men responded to his funny. So he turned to the Montagnard. "Goddamned tiger-boy bastard. You betrayed me."

The Montagnard replied in French, "I understand your anger, Karl."

"You don't understand shit, tiger boy." Zavello, his hands tied at the wrists with nylon cord, sat in a black leather wing chair. He rubbed his face.

"My eye patch."

"You lost it in the forest. I carried you over my shoulder."

"So." That was why his face felt as if he had gone through a car wash with his head stuck out the window. He must have been slapped silly by the branches and tall grass. He stared at the skinny Montagnard, wondering how the slight figure could have carried him so far.

The Montagnard read his mind. "I dragged you most of the way. You're heavier than you used to be."

Zavello shook his head. "Why?"

"The easy life? Too much rich food?"

Zavello had to laugh. "You always were a smart-ass rat bastard, tiger boy. I meant, why the betrayal?"

The Montagnard shrugged. "You want to talk betrayal? America left Vietnam thirty years ago." He gave Zavello a hard stare. "America left the South Vietnamese. America left the Montagnard people, too." He shook his head. "You felt guilty at least about turning your back on the South Vietnamese. But the Montagnard people you never so much as gave your front, let alone your back. Except for the ways we could help you, you paid us no attention at all. Now we are barely a people." He nodded his head toward the third person in the room, a Vietnamese officer about Zavello's age, who sat with them around a cocktail table the size of a large pizza. The fourth and fifth people in the room were armed guards, standing rigid as totem poles at either side of the door. Zavello looked at the officer. The man had no reaction to looking into his vacant, damaged eye socket.

The Montagnard said, "Colonel tat Thant allows my small band to flourish here in the forest. It does not matter to him that we cross into Laos and Cambodia now and then. We keep to the jungle. We do favors for each other. Now and then he pays me. Sometimes in gold, sometimes in surplus rations from his garrison."

Zavello turned to the Montagnard. Snapping his head so quickly was a mistake; he thought his swollen brain might squirt out of his eye socket. The Montagnard turned his head aside as well. Not from the sight of his eye, but because Zavello realized he had an edge. Of course, the Vietnamese colonel didn't know that the Montagnard had been in on the raid against the missile, and probably didn't know that the Vietnamese sentry had been killed.

Zavello looked around the room. "The tiger. Where's that damned tiger?"

"Outside the camp. He doesn't like to be confined. He also finds that other people do not understand him. Besides, he has something of a distaste for the Vietnamese." He inclined his head toward the colonel. "Unfortunately, he won't even eat them."

Zavello narrowed his good eye and stared. The Montagnard would not look back at him.

The Vietnamese colonel shifted in his chair. "Enough of this woman's chatter."

He spoke English better than the Montagnard. Zavello was surprised at first. Then he remembered why that might be possible. "Prisoners. You're keeping Americans as prisoners."

"No," said tat Thant.

"This isn't a prison camp? My men see otherwise. They have pictures."

Tat Thant pooched his lips and cocked his head over his left shoulder. "It might seem so. Yes, we have the wire and the security detachment. But nobody in our community wants to leave, except for the guards who ask for transfers to the city garrisons now and then. It is lonely duty out here."

Zavello laughed, baring his teeth, leaning forward in his chair, despite the feeling that his head would fall off his shoulders and roll onto the floor. He wanted to stick his face closer to the Vietnamese colonel.

"You don't see the contradiction in that? Wires and guards, but nobody wants to leave?"

"It is not to debate. The wire is not to keep in the members of our community. It is to keep out intruders." The Vietnamese colonel strained his head above his shoulders. "Intruders like yourself, Colonel Zavello. You are the only inmate behind this wire. And only because you invaded our country."

Whether he believed tat Thant about the Americans did not matter to Zavello. Only that last part. The harsh truth was, he was a prisoner, something he had avoided in three consecutive combat tours in Vietnam, mostly behind enemy lines. The irony disturbed him too much, so he went on a the attack.

"Bullshit. I saw—heard different. My men reported to me that you were about to execute prisoners—"

"We have no prisoners but you."

The little colonel was fast on his feet, Zavello thought. And so articulate in English. "—why the firing squad?"

"That was a ruse. They are alive."

"Bullshit."

"As I say, this is not to debate. It either is, or it isn't."

Zavello decided to press him. "No, you have only said it is."

Tat Thant smiled, his first showing of emotion in the exchange. "Colonel, I see where you are going. You want me to prove it. You must understand. I was educated in your American university system. University of California, in fact. Los Angeles campus. I am well skilled in semantics. The American members of my community have been here for more than three decades, some of them. All of them voluntarily." He raised his eyebrows at Zavello. "They have helped me keep up the English."

"Deserters. Traitors to their own country." He spat the words.

Tat Thant shrugged, cocking his head again. "These men love peace more than they love war, that is all. This led them to leave their military units. Or, in the alternative, once they were captured, it led them to choose another country. It does not matter whether you think them traitors."

Zavello's anger had begun to clear his thinking, like a dose of smelling salts. He knew better than to underestimate the mind of this small colonel. Any more than he would dare to underestimate the body and fighting ability of the Montagnard. He knew damned well he had better be careful from here on out.

Zavello chose his words carefully. "Tell me, Colonel, of all the men ever entrusted to your care, probably many of them prisoners of war, after, say, 1975, did any of them ever attempt to escape any of your camps?"

Tat Thant spoke as carefully as Zavello had. "This is our only community of Americans, our only camp, as you call it." He gave Zavello a wry smile, letting him know that he would give him points for trying to trick him into saying there were more camps. "Nobody has ever asked to leave, although most days the gates are left open. But, of course, ever since you and your committee of intruders destroyed some of our military equipment and killed many innocent soldiers, a price will have to be paid. For a while, we will have to shut our naturalized citizens inside the gates of this community. And you—?"

The last two words gave Zavello a chill. Yes, him. He was

the prisoner of war now. His mind ran its finger down a short list of options.

Tat Thant spoke to him from the same list. "Your country will not send anybody for you, you know. Your capture would be too embarrassing, if made public. Especially with the attack on our military equipment. A convoy of much-needed food was destroyed by your soldiers the other night. That food was intended for the poor people of the highlands, the Montagnards, the—"

"Bullshit."

"I have pictures, sir. I have proof. Unfortunately, the attackers, whose identity might never be discovered, escaped without a trace."

The little colonel was staring at him. Zavello could stare with the best of them; his eye stayed moist most of the time, so he did not have to blink as often as normal people. Now his mouth felt very dry. He wanted to swallow, but he dared not, in case he would gulp. He knew the drill. If they kept him long enough, he could not overcome the effect of becoming devoted to his captors, the Stockholm effect.

"No need to be nervous, Colonel Zavello."

"I'm not nervous." He wished he hadn't said it. The tremble in his voice said otherwise.

Tat Thant gave him a two-eyed wink, as if to say both, *Who's got the two eyes here?* and, *Who's full of bullshit now?*

"You're thinking of the Stockholm effect, in which the kidnapped are so dependent on their kidnappers that they develop a kind of affection for them, a devotion, really?"

"Ah, I get it. Your education. Your English. Your assignment. You were an interrogator, weren't you? During the war. You know the Stockholm effect. You practically invented it."

Tat Thant ignored him. "Did I tell you that I buried my son this week?"

He said it in the tone of: *Did I mention I had rice for*

breakfast this morning? It gave Zavello a chill. He knew what was coming.

"He died from burns he suffered in the diesel fire that you and your men ignited. Unfortunately, I could not go with him to his place of rest. You see, my superiors in Ho Chi Minh City are very concerned with those in charge of security of the food shipment that was lost. Then, with the attack on the community this morning and the loss of so many men, why, you can understand that I am under certain pressures."

Zavello felt as if his heart would thrash its way out of his chest. He worked hard to control himself, clenching his hands together so they would not tremble. He relaxed his diaphragm, so he could breathe normally, slowly, slowly. Never, in all the years that he had spent behind enemy lines, had he ever once considered that he would be taken alive, that he would ever be put inside the place like this. He had vowed that he would die fighting, that he would keep one bullet for himself, to escape capture by the ultimate means.

Yet, here he was. Back inside Vietnam, a place he had never expected to visit again. Except on that impulse at the mention of the name of a friend. No, make that an enemy, dammit. Left with no hope of getting his hands on a bullet, let alone a weapon.

"Well, I think we have accomplished all that we can," tat Thant said. "I suppose you are eager to meet the rest of your new community." He spoke it as matter-of-factly as if to say Zavello had just joined a religious order, the Jesuits or the Moonies.

Zavello squinted at him in disbelief. He knew how awful that expression could be, had in fact, rehearsed in front of the mirror without the patch. When he squinted with his right eye, the glint was a savage enough sight in its own right. But the muscles of the damaged left eyelid formed a triangular door to his head, a gateway to a pink, moist ball of cotton candy. He had made people puke with that expression. But not this guy.

Not tat Thant. Zavello's stomach sank. This man had seen—had done—more horrible things than look into a vacant eye socket. He had probably plucked many an eye himself. Probably with the fingers of his bare hands, easy as peeling a soft-boiled egg with his fingers.

"We should go now," tat Thant said.

Zavello stood up, thinking how odd it was that neither the Vietnamese nor the Montagnard had made any but the most indirect mention of the Force Recon team outside the wire. Of course, he had not either. Not that it mattered. They all three were playing poker, but with the same hole card. All three knew that the team would be coming for Zavello.

NIGHT RUNNER LED them straight through the center of the clearing outside the camp, finding it not so clear, after all. The deep grasses, far more dense than the forest, towered over their heads, shutting them in completely, except for the patch of sky directly overhead. They walked in file pressing down the grasses. Night Runner had decided to walk directly into the wind. The helicopter waited at idle on a ridgeline, not more than thirty minutes away. On Swayne's command, the pilots would reposition to another landing zone about five minutes' flying time from the camp and wait again. Once he took off, he would barely have time to get up to airspeed before landing here. Blazing a path in the deep grass would help the pilot line up his approach.

Just beyond the center of the clearing, Night Runner stopped and let the others catch up. There was little point in putting out security, but Swayne had another purpose in mind when he sent Greiner and Friel out on opposite, perpendicular lines. They were to walk back and forth, creating a cross in the beaten grass. Finally, he and Night Runner followed each other, walking in a circle, spiraling outward to create an open space, a miniature crop circle. It didn't need to be big enough for a helicopter to land on. Just large enough to see from the sky as the intersection of the cross, a touchdown point. The rotor wash of the helicopter would push the grasses down. This space was to make room for the team, Zavello, and any other people that they would bring out of the camp.

SWAYNE HAD TO smile at himself in the dark. They had damned little chance of bringing out Zavello, let alone anybody else. This was a mission impossible. Chances were good that they weren't even going to get into the camp. They would be calling that helicopter in for themselves. They would be running for their lives, chased by up to a battalion of Vietnamese soldiers. It didn't matter whether they were experienced or not. If their officers could run along behind them, lashing their backs, yelling and encouraging, the Vietnamese could overpower the Spartans by sheer numbers. Ragtag fighters had proven that time and time again. The last time in Somalia against Army Rangers and Delta Force operators.

Swayne wasn't fond of making all the noise that was required to tramp through the grass, although he doubted the sounds could be heard except from directly overhead.

He and Night Runner had sketched a rough plan before they left the staging area. On the march down, he had tried to give it some shape and polish. He went over it again with Night Runner, who added one significant embellishment. It seemed an idea right out of the movies. Swayne couldn't help liking it. Something so outrageous was bound to work. For the first time in hours, he felt confident. For the first time since he could remember, he felt a sense of hope that he might actually find out something about his father.

He decided to forsake security, again because of something Night Runner had told him about hiding in the grass. "The grouse and the pheasant in Montana. They sleep among the dry grasses and the low bushes. Nothing, not even a fox, can sneak up without making noise.

With his team around him, Swayne felt whole. On a mission he seldom had the entire group together in one spot. They had always stayed dispersed. They were often on separate, supporting missions. He signaled for them to shut off their microphones. What he was about to tell them, he did not want the anal retentive officer in the OMCC to hear.

When he had finished the five paragraph field order, Friel had only one thing to say about the mission, the ultimate Friel compliment: "Shit-fire."

Greiner just stared.

"What is it, Corporal?"

"Sir, you really think we can sneak some prisoners out of there?"

"We're going to try. It's the one thing that would prove to the world that the Vietnamese have others. If we can get a handful of men out, maybe, just maybe, international pressure will help others get out."

"Right," Friel said. "Maybe the French will help."

Swayne did not react to that. He knew one thing for dead-solid sure: small as the chances were, if his father was inside that camp, he was not going to leave it to diplomats and politicians to extract him. These men, these Spartans would be the ones.

"We have a few hours before the camp is asleep. We'll go on minimum security here. One on, three off. Try to get some rest. I couldn't sleep right now anyhow. I'll take the first watch. Give me your PDAs so I can program them."

Swayne lay on one elbow for a long time, listening for the breathing of his men to become regular and slow. Friel drifted off first. Then Greiner. Night Runner, he couldn't hear. The man was not even a whisper of sight or sound.

Swayne put his mind to the timetable, running down the plan again and again, looking for places where it could go wrong. There were plenty of holes. He tried to develop alternative courses of action along the way, until one course of action melded into another. As good as he was at making sense of chaos, even he sometimes got confused.

He realized it wasn't because the plan was so confusing. It was because his heart was so confused. The first watch passed, and he took a second, Greiner's. Then came Friel's. Then Night Runner's.

Not five minutes into it, Night Runner stirred and came to his side. Again Swayne was amazed at how quiet Night Runner could be moving across the grass, dry and crackling as it was. Why didn't the laws of physics apply to him as well as to everybody else? He had only met one man—he would not even think about the Bedouin. It was disloyal to Night Runner to think that somebody might be better, although he'd seen that Runner himself worried about the Montagnard.

Again, they turned off their microphones. "You can't sleep." A declaration, not a question.

Swayne shook his head, knowing the man could see him somehow, even without his night vision goggles. "It's a complicated plan."

Night Runner nodded. He understood both the statement and the meaning behind the words. He checked his watch.

It gave Swayne a thought. "Should we move closer to the camp? Get the lay of the land?"

Night Runner grunted. He went to awaken the others. Before they left, Swayne ran over the plan again, especially their extraction instructions. In case they got split up in the confusion of battle, he wanted everybody to be able to take a straight shot toward this spot in the landing zone.

"I'm going to leave a PERLOBE here," he told everybody. "The pilot has the freq. Each of you should dial it in. I'm going to leave it active. While you were asleep I programmed each of your PDAs so you could get back here without hitting the booby traps we left this morning."

They rose as one and fell into march order, Night Runner in the lead. Swayne had long ago lost count of individual missions. Only one thing could he be sure of: never had he been so jittery as this on any of them, not even the first.

ZAVELLO FOUND HIMSELF staring into dozens of angry faces. Men clearly Americans, Asian women, and mixed-race children. Vietnamese officers and soldiers with weapons. Not a friendly face in the lot.

"You see my problem, don't you, Colonel Zavello?" tat Thant asked. "I am not the only one to have lost a child today."

He walked into the group and brought three reluctant men forward. "I don't know if you can recognize these men. They volunteered to be the object of our fake firing squad today. As you can see, they have come to no harm. They are good actors, no?"

Zavello did not betray any surprise or acknowledge that he knew of the attempted executions captured on video by the Spartans.

"You must forgive the weapons, Colonel. Usually, my men do not carry them. These are only for your protection."

"Protection from what?"

"The families have—shall we say, issues—with you and your soldiers. Several of them received wounds today from the firefight. Many of the American men asked to be given weapons to shoot back at you."

Now that was too much. "I don't believe it."

A tall American wearing an orange beard frosted with white stepped forward. "It's true. I would have shot you. If somebody left you alone with me, I would kill you now."

Zavello looked to tat Thant. He raised one eyebrow—the one over his injured eye—and said to the Vietnamese officer, "I'd like that. Leave us alone. I'd be happy to meet with everyone in this room, one on one." He did not shout. He did not even raise his voice. He spoke simply and earnestly. "Come on, Colonel, leave us alone."

The colonel laughed as if Zavello had made a great joke.

"That won't be possible, either. In spite of your attacks, we are a peaceful community here. In time, you will be at peace as well. Tonight, we're simply going to get acquainted. You must listen to the grievances of our people."

Zavello fought his impulses. He wanted to tear into tat Thant, then go for the traitors. That was ridiculous, and he knew it. First, for the obvious reason that the Montagnard would bash the other side of his head before he could even get close to the colonel. Second, because these Americans, no matter what their reasons for deserting or going over to the enemy, could hardly be blamed for what had happened in more than thirty years of brainwashing.

Zavello put on his most civilized face, although he had none that could quite qualify as civilized. He turned and spoke to the group, searching deep within himself to find his most polite tone of voice, a tone that he would have to fake, since it did not come to him naturally.

"Please, I have just one question. I promise that I will be on my best behavior. I will listen to your grievances and try to answer them. I am sorry for any harm that has come to you or your families here. I am sorry that I have behaved badly both today and in the past. But just answer me this one question. Please. Is there anybody in this group by the name of Jack Swayne?"

NIGHT RUNNER WATCHED from the trees, as he had this morning. He checked his wristwatch. Make that *yesterday* morning. He was in a position to watch the camp, of course. But he was just as concerned with the camp's defenses. He studied the obstacles in order. He looked for all the measures that could be used against him. He watched for the routine of the guards.

Earlier, he had left the Spartans where the grasses dissolved into the undergrowth at the margin of the jungle. He used his scimitar as quietly as he could to approach the camp, cutting small branches and leaves, each stroke like a caress of the keen blade. When they left, they would have to be on the run. This would make it easier to see, a tunnel through the foliage. Except for the last thirty meters. From there, he carefully bent over the saplings and pushed twisted branches out of the way, tucking them behind trees when necessary to clear the path. Then he went back and brought the team forward, guiding them into a position about a hundred meters from where he and Friel had struck at the camp earlier. There, where all the shooting had gone on through the wire, was the best position to launch a breakout.

He had found the key while lying in the trees, studying the camp. In a way, it was almost too simple.

First, he went forward to plant concussion grenade charges at the base of two trees nearest the wire, not ten meters from the first obstacle, the crisscrossed netting of barbed wire at ankle height. He would be the one to go to inside the camp and get the prisoners ready to leave. On his signal, Swayne would start the third firefight of the day, this one near the main gate, drawing the garrison's defenders and any outside reaction force.

Swayne had already pinpointed a small refueling tanker parked inside the wire. The Vietnamese probably used the fuel for the camp's trucks, heating, and cooking. The Spartans would use it as an offensive weapon. Once soldiers reacted to prevent an escape or a breach of the sally ports, Friel would touch off the tanker with his 20 mm, adding to the confusion and subtracting from the numbers of defenders.

From inside the camp, Night Runner would blow the two trees, the charges set to make them fall toward the defenses, pressing down on the wire, knocking out all the obstacles for a space of twenty meters. The branches would also set off any remaining flares and mines, creating yet more confusion.

Night Runner had spotted the most significant defensive blunder inside the camp, as well. A tall tree very close to the wire, capable of being felled so that its trunk lay between the two trees knocked down from the opposite direction.

Night Runner might lead Zavello and as many as half a dozen other prisoners across the bridge formed by the tree trunks. Covering fire from Greiner and Friel would prevent anybody from following until they cleared the area. Then everybody would recover to the helicopter LZ.

Simple as that.

Lying in the crown of his tree, nearly fifty feet off the ground, Night Runner granted himself a silent but hearty laugh. How many simple plans had he seen blow up in the team's face? It wasn't only the best-laid plans that went awry, or even the complicated ones. It was basically any plan.

The first sign of Zavello came from the building that he and Swayne had already identified as the living quarters for prisoners. A flash of yellow lit up the courtyard as a door opened, then closed behind five men.

Night Runner identified them all, if not by name, then by occupation. He trained his rifle scope on the group and made sure it was in video mode. Zavello walked between the Montagnard and a man clearly an officer, from his carriage, age, and demeanor perhaps the camp commander. Behind the trio walked a pair of guards armed with rifles.

Night Runner had expected to have to break into the only building that looked like it was capable of holding prisoners, the shack with bars, its walls draped with concertina.

Instead, the group went into the administration building. Half an hour later, lights began to go out inside the building.

At the front of the building, Night Runner had already seen signs of a watch officer. There were probably noncoms and administrative people as well. The living quarters appeared to be at the rear of the building. Where would they keep Zavello? In a closet? A holding cell? In a chair surrounded by guards?

Night Runner waited for the camp to go to sleep. He wished he might go to sleep himself. He did not want to go inside that building. He did not want to face the Montagnard in battle, except perhaps from a distance, where he felt sure he could outshoot the man with his superior rifle and night sights. He chided himself for the lapse in self-confidence. The Montagnard was not the only man in the world capable of more stealth than he in the forest. There were no doubt plenty of others. Among the Montagnard people, probably all of the men and half of the women and children were more stealthy. Never had he needed to psych himself for a mission. This time, though, he gave himself a pep talk before setting out, reminding himself that his high-tech toys would compensate for whatever he lacked in the ability to tiptoe through the forest. The thin man might have the superior senses, but Night Runner had the tools that would put him in front at the finish.

Right? Right!

He checked his watch. Whether he was right or merely working a cheap motivational trick on himself, the time had come to set matters in motion.

Already Night Runner had lightened his load as much as possible. Back at the staging area in the grass, he had distributed his gear and ammunition to the other members of the team. Greiner carried his Brat, with its superior firepower. He had given his sensitive equipment, the PDA and the PER-LOBE to Swayne—as much as he had come to rely on them. In fact he carried—and wore—almost nothing into the tree with him. A rope. His scimitar, its sheath taped to the center of his back with some of the team's bad-ass duct tape. He had removed his 9 mm holster from his belt and taped it to his ribs beneath his left pectoral muscles. In a fanny pack strapped to his waist, he carried a minimum of supplies: a roll of the bad-ass tape, three concussion grenades, and the remote detonator. He wore only his camouflaged briefs, not even the soft-skin boots.

Across his body, he draped a coil of rope. He had taken the fifty-foot length of cord from the pack of each team member and used them to braid a thicker length of rope. Something he could get a grip on.

He adjusted his night vision goggles and began his treacherous journey. Weaving left and right, climbing up and down, he traveled the irregular treetop highway. Always searching for branches that would support his weight, he walked among the tangled limbs, careful not to break twigs and drop them to the rooftops below. It took him most of an hour to cross the wire, traveling fifty to eighty feet above it. Once, he had to balance precariously, turn, and backtrack, after walking out onto a branch, expecting to be able to reach up to another limb to continue his way. But his weight had made the branch sag, and he couldn't get to it. Instead, he had to climb thirty feet, find an even slimmer branch above, let it sag under his weight, hang by his fingers, reaching with his toes. Even at that, he came up three feet short. He cursed himself for not taking time to lower himself with the rope. He decided not to backtrack and, watching through his night vision binoculars, swung clear, released the upper branch, and grabbed onto the lower branch as he fell by, hoping that it would not snap and give him away or drop him into the wire, where he would be found and shot.

The branch held. He swung hand to hand, branch to branch, until he could throw a leg up and gather himself for a rest. As he did so, a snag caught his night vision binoculars and tore them off his head. He grabbed for them, nearly losing his balance. His fingers closed on a wire. Below him he heard a metallic tinkle as the binoculars fell into the tallest coils of concertina.

The wire he had saved was his radio mike, but the radio had fallen as well. Night Runner waited for his heart rate to slow down so he could hear something besides his pulse in his ears.

Apparently he had triggered no alarms and had not alerted any of the camp's sentries. Still, he waited an extra twenty minutes for his natural vision to adjust to the darkness. By definition, the night vision goggles sent a brightened picture to his eyes and washed out his ordinary night vision for a while. He was sorry, sorry that he'd let his fear of the Montagnard's prowess make him doubt himself, sorry that he had relied so much on machines.

Once he started moving again, Night Runner was surprised at how much he could see. He promised himself that, in the future, he would not rely so much on high-tech devices. If he were to get out of this situation, he would train his night vision, adapting to the dark like an animal.

THE MONTAGNARD WATCHED the American breach the camp's defenses like a climbing cat. Just twenty-four hours ago, he had made his own way into the camp like a python, keeping to the ground. Someday he would have to try the American's way, through the trees. He was sure he could do it faster. He might even try it by daylight, since the Vietnamese seemed never even to consider the canopy as a way into the camp. In fact, he'd never even seen a guard look up into the trees—the threat for them would come through the wire, always the wire. He himself had not considered the trees as a way in. He gave the American grudging credit and felt the first twinge of doubt about his utter superiority over the foreigner. The man called Night Runner had showed creativity that the Montagnard had not anticipated. Still, the Montagnard reassured himself, he was better in the forest. Yes, he would always be better. This was his forest. This was his home. He lived here every day, while the American was only a visitor.

Even so, he could not help feeling a moment of distress. For he had not seen the American until he had already crossed over the wire, traveling through the trees. He might not have seen him yet, if his daring jump had not brought down a fluttering cloud of leaves.

He did not react yet. He needed to wait for the other Americans to come inside the camp before he sounded the alarm that would bring out more than a hundred men. Some of the

Vietnamese slept two to a bunk in the quarters of the camp cadre, at least fifty. A like number had found space on the floor of the dining hall. More than two hundred were asleep sitting upright inside trucks less than a quarter mile away.

All waiting for his alarm, which he would sound as soon as he could get a fix on the other three Americans.

NIGHT RUNNER SLIPPED the coils of his braided rope from his head and shoulder. He tied it to the limb and began feeding it to the ground. Like everything else the team carried, a camouflaged pattern, in jungle shades, would hide the rope by day. At night, somebody would have to literally walk into it to know it was there. So he tried to leave its running end off the ground, about seven feet, as near as he could tell from above.

He had shifted his feet into position to lower himself when it struck him. Only a feeling, but a strong one, a big chill, real as a tap on the shoulder.

Crouching, he looked back toward the trunk of the tree. A blur of motion caught his eye. Even as he reached for his pistol, he realized the figure meant no threat toward him. It beckoned him, one sweeping motion of the arm, a motion that ended with the figure's hand beneath his chin.

Night Runner put a hand to his chest. *Me?* The figure beckoned him again. Night Runner knew he could not refuse. No matter that he was in the middle of a mission. Feeling his legs tremble, he stood up to answer the figure's call. He steeled himself, settling his nerves and his muscles. Then he began walking along the limb, using no handholds, not looking down. He did not dare to take his eyes from the figure, fearful that he might disappear.

Yet, when he reached the tree trunk, the figure moved away from him. As he reached the tree trunk, the figure stepped around it. Night Runner followed the figure. But when he stepped around the tree trunk onto another limb, the figure was gone. Night Runner rubbed his eyes. Was he having hallucinations? He looked around. No. Fifty feet away, standing at the same level in another tree, the figure beckoned to him again. Then, as Night Runner watched him, the figure vanished. Again, Night Runner rubbed his eyes. Had he lost his mind?

He pressed his back against the tree, feeling the sheath of his scimitar. He closed his eyes, the better to recollect what had happened in the last few minutes, the better to make sense of things. Was it a phantom? A ghost? Obviously, yes. Because he recognized the face of the figure. It was his own face. And his own body—at least the figment of a body—of a Blackfeet warrior in battle paint. He saw his namesake, his ancestor, Heavy Runner. Here in the forest, he had experienced a vision.

How could that be? No, that was not the question. He had seen the vision. It was. Simple as that. The question was not how. The question was why.

Just as important was the question of the mission. Zavello depended on him. Swayne and the team needed him to do his part. The prisoners could not be freed without him. Yet that image of Heavy Runner beckoned. He could not discount it.

Night Runner realized that his mission and the vision did not have to be disconnected. In fact, the reality and the unreality were tied together. He had walked a good ten meters—thirty feet—along the limb of a rough tree, feeling his way among twigs, branches, leaves, knots, and splinters. He had walked almost as if he had the ability to see with his feet.

He had never experienced that power before, had never even suspected its existence until he'd seen it, in the person of the Montagnard, a man who could know there was a snake at his feet in the dark. He had done it. Somehow he had mastered the skill of the Montagnard.

The reality of Night Runner's sudden sharpening of the senses was no accident. Heavy Runner had beckoned him for a reason. The figure was trying to reassure him that his powers were equal to that of the Montagnard. Something else. Heavy Runner had been trying to tell him something else about the Montagnard, too. But what?

THE MONTAGNARD FELT a smile ease across his face when he saw the American stand up and give a hand signal in the direction from which he had come. That could only mean one thing. Although he couldn't see them, one or more of the Marines had followed the naked one through the treetops. Now he knew that he could sound the alarm the moment the last of the Marines dropped to the ground.

A few seconds later, he grew concerned, and his smile began to dissolve. He had watched the Marines in the forest. They did as well as any white man he had ever known, almost as good as Zavello when he was young and in his prime during the war against the North. But they were not so good that they could have climbed to the trees like the American warrior in bare feet. He had seen their feet, in fact—at least the feet of the youngest man as he changed into dry socks. They were soft, too soft. With no calluses, one could never walk through the trees without boots. Even if only one of them traveled with boots, he would have heard noise by now. He would have seen broken twigs and many more fluttering leaves.

So who had the American been signaling to?

A second concern. Where was he now? For a moment, the Montagnard felt a twinge of alarm. He thought he might even fire his rifle, sounding the general alarm, bringing out reinforcements. He did not. He could not make a fool of himself in front of tat Thant and so many men. They thought he was a superior being, almost a ghost of the forest. He dared not let them see him as a mere mortal.

Still, he wondered. Where was the American?

• • •

ONCE HE CAME to an understanding of why Heavy Runner had showed himself, Night Runner had moved as quickly and silently as an owl, practically flying through the foliage. After seeing Heavy Runner, a variation in the original plan came to Night Runner, and he would have liked his radio to tell Swayne and the others of his deviation. But that was no longer possible.

He had climbed the tree another thirty feet and crossed through the network of branches to the spot where Heavy Runner had last stood before he disappeared for good. Then, rather than using a rope, Night Runner went down the tree trunk, quiet as a cat. Once on the ground, he wasted no time.

Night Runner felt as if he had been injected with new hope, new confidence, new powers. His senses and his awareness had grown in acuity. He could hear the sounds of the night more sharply than before. He could hear men snoring in the dining hall, easily ten meters away. He could hear a quiet shuffling of boots inside the administration building, no doubt a walking sentry. What's more, he could hear a voice in his head telling him what to look for and how to adjust his plan.

He could see much better now than with the night vision goggles, better because his field of view was not confined to the narrow screen that saw only in the direction he turned his head. He could see farther and wider. What's more, he could look beyond the present. He could see himself in a vicious battle, one that would cause him great harm.

He could touch. But more important, he could feel with an extra-sharp sense that included perception well beyond ordinary touch.

He wrapped a pair of concussion grenades around the base of the tree, both set to the same frequency, both intended to knock the tree down over the wire from inside the camp.

Then he moved to the administration building. He pressed his body against the wall, feeling the cold stucco on his chest. He listened with one ear pressed to the wall, both palms soaking up vibrations, his skin drawing conclusions about what was inside, his nose and mouth picking up scent molecules like the forked tongue of the snake, testing them, sorting, cataloging, deciding. The sum of all his senses, although his eyes were closed, gave him a crisp picture of what lay beyond this wall.

It could not have been more clear if Heavy Runner had gone into the building to scout it, to relay psychic pictures to him.

He measured the walking posts by the sound of the sentry's stopping points. Back and forth along a hallway. Night Runner moved along the wall until he was at the midpoint of the walking post. Then he heard—or, rather, saw on the screen of his new sensitivity—a second man. This one stood, shifting his weight from one foot to the other, sending a vibration through the floorboards to Night Runner.

Beyond this second man, Night Runner could hear the breathing of a third man: Zavello. He knew the sound from the nights they had spent together in the forest. These were short breaths and rapid. The colonel had not fallen asleep. What was more, he was afraid.

Night Runner traveled from one end of the hallway to another, keeping pace with the sentry, stopping when the man pivoted to go back. He listened, felt, touched, tasted, smelled. In this way, he discovered another man at the end of the hallway, sitting in a chair that creaked. When the sentry returned, Night Runner walked with him on his post back to the other extent of his trip, about twenty feet in all. Another sentry, also sitting in a chair. This one asleep.

He knew all this in less than a minute. In much less than that, he had decided how to take down the position. With his final strip of bad-ass duct tape, he fastened his last concussion grenade, its hinge left open, so the flat sides of each half sphere would rest against the building.

He crept to the front of the administration building, drawing both his 9 mm pistol from its holster and his remote-control detonator. At the front porch, he walked boldly, so the Spartans could see him, but quietly, so the enemy inside could not hear him. He crouched beside the steps up to the front, his pistol at the ready. A moment of doubt flashed through his head. Was it really Heavy Runner he had seen? A true vision? Or a mere figment of his own imagination? Was he acting on facts? Or dreams?

Only several things could he know for certain: he had achieved a heightened sense of awareness; either from a warning of the spirits in the vision or because of his own intuition, he had decided on a change in plan; and now, for better or worse, it was up to him to set off the next sequence in the chain of events that would either set free Zavello and the other prisoners—or kill them.

Fact was, he trusted the vision of Heavy Runner more than his own intuition. At least the vision, it seemed, had been trying to warn him about the Montagnard. Without ever giving him a direct sign that going down the rope would lead to danger, the figure in the vision had led him away from the rope. His own intuition hadn't done as well. He had lost track of the Montagnard. For all he knew, the man was watching him. Or perhaps waiting for him inside the administration building, perhaps even inside Zavello's cell.

In that one respect, all his senses had failed him. He could not see, hear, smell, taste, or touch the Montagnard. Yet he could not help but feel fearful that the thin man who had betrayed the team now was in a position to watch, listen, smell, taste, and touch him at will. He could not resist the urge to turn around in a full circle. A small chill began working its way down his spine, the feeling that he was a target. Such a feeling was so unfamiliar to him that he gave in to its urging, almost in panic, setting off the first concussion grenade.

SWAYNE HAD CAUGHT his first glimpse of Night Runner a few seconds after seeing the rope dropped quietly and carefully like a spider at the one end of its own drop string. He had followed the rope upward and caught the movement of Night Runner walking like a circus performer back toward the tree. He had watched and waited, his night vision binoculars on full power, but saw nothing again. Now and then he would check the rope to see if it had been disturbed by Night Runner sliding down after having somehow gotten past his line of view. Nothing. Swayne had only picked up the gunny again by accident, as he swung his binoculars along the fence line, scanning for a sentry or a patrol. There he saw Runner taping grenades to the base of a tree different from the one they had briefed together. Swayne never gave it a thought that Night Runner had selected the wrong tree. Something had made him change his plan, something important enough for an adjustment but not so important that he needed to make a report.

For a minute, Night Runner disappeared behind the administration building. Swayne saw him next move to the front porch, turn around and hunker down. Somehow Night Runner had lost his night vision goggles. And his radio set.

No problem. It was SOP, standard operating procedure, that setting off the explosion was its own signal to start the attack from outside the wire.

Swayne opened his mike to warn the others. But before he could speak, a flash-bang explosion blew out the windows of the building and threw open the front door.

THE MONTAGNARD HAD seen enough of nothing to know that something had gone wrong. Somehow, lying in his spot beneath the steps to the prisoners' living area, the enemy had spotted him. Otherwise, why would he abandon the rope? The Montagnard had crawled forward and gotten to his feet, intending to run across the open area to the administration building. He had barely shifted his weight forward when the blast hit.

The shock wave did not affect him so much as his own

instincts. He flattened on the ground, barely feeling the sting on his bare skin, struck by bits of wood and glass. More debris sang by, bouncing off the walls of the building.

Somehow the American named Night Runner had discovered him. He had found a way to the ground and sneaked down from the trees. He hadn't expected his enemy to set the charge to the building where their commander was being held prisoner. Above all, more than the explosion, he had lost track of three of the Americans. That shook him the worst.

Still, there would be time to prevent anybody inside the camp from escaping. He got to his hands and one knee when another, louder explosion went off, this time outside the wire. This time, the Americans started shooting with small arms. Now he knew for certain that he had been fooled. Only one American had come inside. None was in the trees. The others were attacking from outside the wire. How? How had the naked American spotted him?

A third explosion, more distant, meant that the fuel tankers had been struck near the gate.

The Montagnard wondered whether the Americans had sent in another, larger force to assist the Marines. Otherwise, how could there be so much firepower?

Already he heard shouting from inside the dining hall and the quarters of the garrison troops. He needed to act quickly. Once those green troops burst out of their buildings and were met by gunfire from the Americans, they were going to shoot at anything that moved. He gained his feet and thought he would run across the open area, diving into the space beneath the floor of the building and the ground.

But once the shooting began from outside the wire, he decided to hold his position beneath the prisoners' building. The Americans would not shoot it up, and the naked American would almost certainly try to lead his colonel toward the front gate—there was no other way to get through the wire.

He let off the safety of his rifle and waited for the pair to come out of the administration building. It was a disappointment to him that he would not be able to help capture the entire American force. But he would be able to kill the American Indian. His companion, the tiger, would do the same to one or more of the enemy outside the wire. The Vietnamese would pay him handsomely for the fighters he had brought them. The colonel would be a prize, but these Marines, these warriors were even more precious.

NIGHT RUNNER WAITED a few seconds between the first explosion and toppling the pair of trees across the wire. He wanted to hear from the stunned men inside the administration building. Would they run toward the explosion at the middle of the building, trying to prevent the attack? Or would they run out the front door?

The Vietnamese answered his question soon enough, stumbling out onto the porch, running away from the building, leaving their weapons behind.

He let three of them go by. They called out to each other as they ran, shouting because the explosion had deafened them. They drew attention to themselves running across the yard and went down in a blast of machine gun fire from outside the wire.

Night Runner leapt onto the porch, stepping carefully in his bare feet to avoid the broken glass. Bent low, he ducked into the dusty, smoky building. Once inside, he touched off the second explosion, bringing down the pair of trees across the fence line.

He found the door to the hallway, blown down by the blast.

"Montagnard," he yelled, the French word for mountaineer, hoping that his near-naked appearance and the word would keep him from getting shot. He yelled it because anybody in this hallway would be deafened.

Lying on top of the door was an unconscious—or dead—

Vietnamese sentry. Night Runner stepped around him and bent low, calling, "Colonel, are you in there? Colonel Zavello, can you hear me?"

Squatting low, Night Runner did the duck walk like a recruit in boot camp. He could not see to the opposite end of the hallway for the dust. He could not hear anything, either, because of the firefight outside, which grew in intensity by the second. He could visualize Vietnamese soldiers running out into the night, shooting everywhere. They had already showed their lack of discipline in the afternoon's firefight. He heard bullets slapping into the building from several directions and knew they were not all coming from the Spartans.

He reached the spot in the wall where the concussion grenade had gone off. He would have liked a bigger hole, big enough for both him and Zavello, because that was where he intended to leave the building.

A moment of panic struck him when he reached the doorway inside the hallway, the spot where he had identified Zavello's holding cell. A pool of blood ran from the doorway into the hallway, spreading even as he approached. As he got closer, he saw the sandals and legs of a Vietnamese sentry. The man had been next to the outside wall almost exactly where the grenade had gone off. It had blown him into the doorway of Zavello's room, knocking the door off its hinges. In one swift motion, Night Runner stood up and stepped inside the room, calling, "Colonel Zavello—"

A strong arm closed around his throat. "Here I am, you Montagnard bastard."

"No," Night Runner squeaked, dropping his 9 mm pistol so he could try to pry the arm away far enough to speak his own name. He was surprised at how strong the Marine colonel had kept himself. As the crook of Zavello's elbow cut off the blood flow in his neck, he saw sparkles at the edges of his vision. Of course, the man had learned how to apply pressure to stop the blood flow to the brain, then crush the windpipe, making an opponent senseless within seconds, killing him in a minute.

Outside, the gun battle had reached a crescendo, but the loudest sound was that of his heartbeat inside his own head. Night Runner raised an elbow to throw back into Zavello's ribs. He needed to get free, to tell him that he was a Marine, not a Montagnard.

But before he could throw the blow, Zavello released him. "Night Runner? Gunny?"

Night Runner massaged his throat to restore the circulation as quickly as possible, turning to face the colonel, whose back was to the door. "How did you know?"

"You got that toad sticker strapped to your back." Zavello snickered. "Besides, you don't stink like a garlic factory that got fish guts spilled all over—"

Night Runner with a finger to his lips and bent down to find the 9 mm. The squeal he heard might just have been an audio illusion, or a wild ricochet from the firefight outside. But he dared not dismiss his senses. Night Runner bent down, keeping his eyes on the doorway, looking for the dropped 9 mm with his fingertips.

"Monty," Zavello bayed, yelling through his own deafness. "He betrayed us. He's in the camp."

Night Runner felt a stab of fear. *The Montagnard? He might have to fight the Montagnard?* He wasn't ready yet.

He did not need the second squeal to tell him that somebody was in the hallway, perhaps the thin man himself. A figure stepped into the doorway, swinging a pistol, firing twice. Night Runner lunged from his coiled position on the floor, driving beneath the firing hand, aiming his forehead at the man's soft spot between his sternum and pubic bone.

The contact felt good, hard and effective, driving the air from the man's lungs, throwing him against the wall, at the edge of the hole where the concussion grenade had gone off. Night Runner worked his feet, driving, driving, unsure of where the pistol was until he felt it dropped, hitting him in the buttock and falling to the floor. Still he kept pushing, hearing the wood crackle, throwing the man through the hole, following him to the ground. He raised a fist, knuckles extended, ready to drive them into the man's throat.

It wasn't necessary. A splinter of wood, long as a bayonet, had driven through the man's neck from the back and protruded from his face beneath his cheekbone. A gargle came out of the mouth, but no words. Night Runner recognized him. The camp commander.

He turned back toward the hole in the wall as one leg came through. Zavello. He was coming out feetfirst, backing through the hole, which was now a bit wider than before.

"Are you hit, Colonel?"

"Good to go," Zavello bellowed at him, his head still inside the hallway, his hearing shot.

He dragged him through the opening, studying him as he staggered, holding a finger to the man's lips. "Don't try to talk. You have to be quiet."

Night Runner felt the wetness on his hand and rubbed his fingers together, feeling the slime that he knew was blood. "Turn around. You're hit. I want to check out your wound."

"Later. Let's get out of—" he couldn't finish shouting his response, because Runner clapped a hand over his mouth.

"The prisoners—"

Zavello peeled Night Runner's hand away from his lips. "They don't want to be rescued," he brayed.

"The Stockholm—"

"Forget the damned Stockholm effect. The bastards don't want to be rescued. Now, let's get the hell out of here."

"No more talking." Night Runner reached into his waist pack. He wasn't so much worried about talking; the firefight, although it had diminished some, was noisy enough to drown out their words. But if somebody caught even a snatch of English, they would shoot first and sort out the translations later.

Night Runner withdrew Swayne's remote detonator. Two

buttons depressed at once set off the final charges. Even as the lone tree began toppling for the wire from inside the camp, Night Runner called out, *"Allons,"* French for *Let's go.*

Almost at once, they were shielded by shrubs and the garden outside the camp headquarters. Then they were among the tree trunks. Night Runner listened to make sure that Zavello kept up. His breathing sounded strong and clean, not wet, so he knew the colonel had not been struck in the lungs.

He needed Zavello to be steady for the next part of the journey. By now the fighting had concentrated in three main areas: the spot where he knew the dining hall to be, the housing area for the garrison, and the main gate. The tree he had felled was exposed only to the main gate, and from what he could see illuminated by the spreading pool of fire, Friel had hit the fuel truck. Nobody would be able to see through the flames or to come at them from that direction.

He went first out onto the tree trunk. It was an easy walk for him, because his bare feet gave him such good contact and made balancing easy. Ten feet into the fence line, he turned around to check on Zavello's progress. Although the tree trunk was easily two feet in diameter at its base and lay on the ground, Zavello was walking as if it were a tightwire suspended fifty stories above Manhattan during a winter wind storm, his arms wobbly to his sides, his legs like linguine.

Zavello was still dazed. Runner started back to help him across.

Zavello would have none of it. "Go on. Get across."

Night Runner hesitated, but when he saw that Zavello, trying to concentrate on him, became even more unsteady, he turned and sprinted across the tree trunk toward the tangles of wire ahead, hoping to clear the final obstacle before Zavello got there.

At the middle of the highest fence, the coils of concertina had folded around the tree trunk, closing like a healed wound, engulfing the makeshift bridge. Night Runner reached with both hands over his head and pulled his scimitar. When the tree fell, it had broken branches out of other trees, dragging the tangles to the ground. Some of those had fallen free. He whacked through the tree limbs, clearing the path along the tree trunk, picking up several of the pieces and cutting two of them to the height of a man. When he got to the overlapping coils, he used one end of the first pole to push coils aside, then he braced the opposite set of coils with the other end of the first stick. The expedient left enough room for Night Runner to step through with his second stick. This time it was not so easy. The coils had hung up on each other. Much as he did not want to, Night Runner knew there was only one thing to do. Knowing that he might never get its edge back, he swung at the knot of concertina wire with his curved sword. The steel blade amazed him yet another time. He had seen it cut through men and wood. Never had he expected it could sever strands of steel wire. But just as if he were using a machete to chop through banana fronds, the wire came apart. The last tangle broke only with difficulty, so he knew he had used up the scimitar's edge. By the time he had got down his second pole to hold the wires apart, Zavello was upon him, breathing hard, ragged, stressed with the effort of balancing on the tree trunk, but his lungs still sounding dry.

Night Runner could see the look of pain on Zavello's face. He also heard a squishing noise. He looked down and saw that Zavello's left boot had begun leaking blood.

"Move." Zavello didn't have to tell him. Treating the wound would have to wait. Right now, the fuel fire made them stand out like two figures walking in front of a lit movie screen at the theater.

Night Runner turned and ran across the rest of the bridge, stopping just short of where the wire ended to chop at the first branches from the crown of the tree. Once he had cleared a way past the wire, he jumped onto the ground and was relieved to see that Zavello had kept up, although he had begun to stagger.

A voice called to them. Swayne's. Night Runner waited for the colonel, took his hand—his bloody hand—and helped him down. Zavello didn't protest anymore. Night Runner led him toward the voice of the Spartans' leader. Once there among the tree trunks at the edge of the forest, Zavello's knees buckled. Night Runner could see that the loss of blood might make it impossible for him to walk to the LZ.

"Give me your first aid kit," he said. Swayne tossed his pack, and Night Runner found the kit by touch. Everybody on the Spartans team loaded their packs exactly the same way, so anybody digging into any pack in the dark would know where to find such things as ammunition—by caliber— rations, and the first aid kit.

"We have to get going," Zavello gasped.

"First we have to stop the bleeding, so you'll have enough gas to make it to the LZ. Captain, did you call the pickup bird?"

"Affirm. How come no POWs?"

Zavello looked up, as if suddenly remembering. "Your father wasn't there."

Swayne gulped. "What about any other prisoners?" he asked. His weak voice betrayed that he had not really given much thought to any others.

Night Runner turned to see Swayne sag either in relief or disappointment, he couldn't tell which.

"Nobody's coming," Night Runner said. "They wanted to stay."

Swayne whirled as if they were not in the middle of a firefight with perhaps two hundred men.

"They wanted to stay?"

Zavello answered, "Bastards."

Bullets whacked into the foliage around them.

"Is somebody shooting at us? Or is it just wild?" Night Runner asked, shoving a chunk of gauze treated with anticoagulant into Zavello's wound, bringing a groan to the man's lips; but to his credit, he did not say anything.

"Just wild shooting," Swayne said. "Until now." He stood up and extended his rifle around the trunk of a tree to shoot a burst back toward the camp.

"Somebody's coming across your little bridge."

Night Runner said, "I'll toss a boomer. You grab the colonel and take him toward the LZ."

Swayne and Zavello disappeared into the foliage. The captain called for Greiner and Friel to cover their withdrawal and keep contact as they, too, pulled back to the landing zone.

Night Runner found Swayne's pack and oriented it with his hands. He found the right pocket, and went for one of the captain's concussion grenades. He snapped it open and saw that the timer was set to default, 2.5 seconds. As he stood up to throw, he saw the Montagnard high-stepping across the makeshift bridge that he had dropped. He wished he had a rifle. He could end his self-doubts with a single shot.

The grenade would have to do. If he tossed it right, it would put the man out of action. Even if it did not kill him, when he awoke, he would have to concede that he had been beaten.

He opened the hinge, touched the buttons to prearm, and closed the grenade for throwing. He put his thumb over the release button and drew back his arm. The timer would begin the instant he released the button, which worked like pulling the pin on conventional grenades.

Instead of throwing the grenade, he flattened on the ground, warned by his newly sharpened senses, in particular, his sense of smell.

He felt the air disturbed as a body flew over him. He knew what it was by the size, the speed, and especially that smell.

He stood up into the wake of the tiger, rancid and strong. The animal, although it had missed, rebounded quickly, wheeling on the spot, turning to come at him again, this time more deliberately.

Night Runner knew he had only fractions of a second. No time to kneel down and find his scimitar, which had saved his life so many other times.

No sense in running. Not two steps would he get before the sweep of claws would hook into his back as the animal took him down.

Nothing to do but face his danger, his only weapon his wits and that concussion grenade in his right hand. It seemed useless. The animal was too close. If Night Runner set off the grenade, it would kill him, too. If he dropped it and ran, the tiger would leap beyond it and be on him too quickly.

The animal bunched itself for a leap, and Night Runner decided how he must act if he had even the slimmest chance of saving his life. Although it might cost him almost as much.

To his right, he knew that the Montagnard was approaching, armed with a Kalishnakov rifle.

He stared at the animal, waiting to meet the rush. The tiger, though, seemed more than a little reluctant to finish its chase.

Of course! Night Runner remembered from a show on the Discovery Channel; tigers would not attack a man unless they could sneak up from behind. In fact, in the coastal areas of India, the Sunderbans region, tigers accustomed to eating corpses that washed up on shore had become man-eaters. Woodsmen wore masks with large eyes painted on the backs of their heads as they walked through the forest.

He could not turn his back to run.

Not that facing the animal did him much better. The tiger had nailed him to this spot, growling, feinting, swiping at the air between them with huge claws bared, trying to frighten him into bolting. Holding him in this spot as the Montagnard approached with his rifle.

Night Runner began backing into the forest.

"Zavello. Zavello." *The Montagnard was calling to the colonel?* "Come here, Zavello. Where are they, boy?"

No, the Montagnard wasn't calling the Marine officer. He had named his tiger after the one-eyed terror of Force Recon.

Night Runner's heart began to race. He was able to get a few meters into the jungle, but it was tough going because he was unable to see where he was backing. Once he crossed a game trail and thought about taking it because the going would be easier. But then he remembered he had set booby traps on that very trail this morning. If the Vietnamese had not triggered them yet, he might kill himself with his own devices.

The Montagnard kept calling for his tiger, each time his voice getting louder. He might be no more than fifty feet away now, and every time Night Runner turned his head to look for obstacles—something that might trip him up and release the tiger from his gaze—the animal made a rush at him. All he had to do was break eye contact to bring on one of the short, violent charges.

Night Runner knew he had to decide. He had to commit, take a chance. If he did not, the Montagnard would soon be upon him. Once that happened, the contest would be over. One shot from his AK-47 would decide who was the best fighter in the world, no contest at all.

Even if he were closer to the LZ, he could not very well risk the lives of the others by having an attacking tiger leap into the helicopter after him.

"Zavello." The Montagnard had found their trail. He was no more than a dozen paces away.

Night Runner tried one more tactic. He rushed at the tiger. The animal shrank back, its haunches high in the air, its mouth wide open. It would not attack into Night Runner's face, but it would not retreat, either. Perhaps fearful of turning its own back on an attacking enemy.

"There you are, both of you." The voice came from behind and above the tiger.

The great cat did not even look back now. Instead, it grew bolder by the arrival of its companion.

Night Runner's eyes beheld the two leering faces with the same expression, both hungry for the kill.

"So, it has come to this," the Montagnard said in French.

Night Runner did not respond. He knew he could not talk his way out of the situation. There would be no way to put his enemies off guard. And there was no point in chatting. That sort of thing might go on in the movies, but not here, in the jungle, where a firefight still went on, the Vietnamese shooting at each other or blindly into the forest.

Night Runner permitted himself a quick glance beyond the tiger, enough to see that the Montagnard had not raised his rifle to his shoulder.

"You tricked me, you know," the Montagnard said. "But did you know that my tiger is trained to attack on command?"

Night Runner glanced up again, a question in his eyes. Then, feeling the tiger step toward him, closing the distance, he stared back at the animal's eyes, yellow, elongated, eager.

"Oh, yes. Even a frontal attack."

This was it. Night Runner's moment in life that he had always tried to avoid, that instant where all his choices focused on a pinprick of light in an encroaching sphere of darkness. He had one choice, maybe two. Surrender was not on the table. He would not ask for quarter; and they would not give it.

Suicide? He could barely even think the word, let alone get into the assisted suicide that the Montagnard and the tiger would be only too willing to give him.

That left fight or flee, the singular choice in the daily life of the animal kingdom. Flee, he'd already considered and dismissed. Not much different than suicide as a choice.

That left no option except to decide the issue of who among the three would make the first move.

Night Runner saw the barest flicker of movement, the

muzzle of the rifle raising ever so slightly. He lunged.

If the Montagnard had seen his concussion grenade, he didn't let on. Night Runner meanwhile could not forget, his thumb aching from holding down the arm-release button harder than necessary, to make sure he did not start the timing sequence by accident.

His first step surprised both of them. As he switched the grenade from his right hand to his left, the tiger shrank away, and even the Montagnard took a step backward, raising the rifle to defend himself.

Once that grenade was armed, the next two and a half seconds of life were set in motion that could not be changed. With his left hand, Night Runner thrust the grenade at the tiger's maw. With his right, he unstrapped the quick-release buckle of his fanny pack.

He swung the belt, forcing the Montagnard back another step. One second gone. He released the grenade, uncoiling himself for a flying leap to the ground, hoping that the concussion grenade would catch both his enemies standing, while he dove and tried burrowing into the earth like the badger.

In the next second, he realized that his desperate plan had failed. First, the Montagnard flung up his left hand in a defensive gesture and caught the fanny pack as it wrapped around his forearm. He jerked on it, bringing Night Runner a step closer to the armed grenade and the barrel of the rifle.

Even worse, the tiger caught Night Runner's left hand in its jaws, grenade and all. Only Night Runner seemed to realize that the three of them, tied together in a macabre hate triangle, were about to die.

The realization gave him a surge of power. He uncoiled all the strength in his leg muscles, releasing both the fanny pack buckle and the grenade at once. He did dive away, landing flat. He did dig into the foliage, awkwardly and ineffectively. He waited for the sixteen daggers of the tiger to plunge into his back and the four stilettos of its four-inch fangs to pierce his skull.

Instead, he got his heels burned and his back slapped by the concussion of the grenade going off. Then a storm of flesh and blood covered him with its spray. He tried not to think about what it was, as his body tried to lull him into welcoming oblivion.

FRIEL, STANDING WELL outside the rotor wash of the waiting helicopter, was expecting Night Runner to step out of the dark and touch him on his shoulder. The chief always was pulling one of his sneaky Pete tricks like that. Friel would not have minded another one right now. Night Runner had been gone too long. He had never—

The explosion took him by surprise. He recognized it, of course, the louder, brighter blast of the boomers had not yet been duplicated by the French and sold to the outlaw governments and terrorists of the world.

On one hand, he should be relieved. The boomer meant that the gunny was still fighting. On the other hand, Friel felt the oddest premonition. Something had gone wrong. He looked into the black of the forest, staring hard. Suddenly, without asking permission, without even reporting to Swayne, he dashed out of the helicopter landing zone and into the jungle.

ALTHOUGH NIGHT RUNNER had had the good sense to press his face into the rotting foliage on the jungle floor to keep his night vision when the grenade went off, he was stunned and deafened. He knew the symptoms well, but he could not allow himself even a few seconds to try to recover. He rolled over to one elbow, ready to fight.

Not necessary. The tiger was nothing but a carcass—half a carcass, really, its head and forequarters blown away as it absorbed most of the blast. Night Runner looked around, trying to find the Montagnard. A rustling in the branches told him that the thin man had not been killed. Maybe he had leapt aside in reaction to Night Runner's move. Or maybe he had just been bowled over. It didn't matter. He was still alive.

Still, Night Runner felt the flush of victory. He had come as close to death as he had ever expected without actually being killed. Yet he had survived. He had stunned his attacking enemy, cutting the odds in half—more than half. Now he had choices. Moments earlier, his situation had been all but hopeless. Now he saw a way out. All he had to do was get to his feet and start moving. Find the fence. Make his way through the tall grass toward the center of the clearing, where the helicopter would be waiting, blades turning in the landing zone.

He rolled to his knees, ready to push himself to his feet, and fell on the left side of his face. His left hand hurt. It had given way on him. With his right he reached for it, to check how badly the tiger's bite had damaged him. He found nothing. Nothing.

The hand was gone, bitten off by the tiger.

His forearm spurted, and he knew that he had not won, after all. The thought of living without his left hand did not bother him so much as knowing if he did not get assistance at once, he would not be living at all.

"Zavello," the Montagnard murmured. He was stunned but thrashing through the bushes toward Night Runner.

Night Runner grabbed the stump of his left forearm, thinking, *The stump?* He gripped it, digging his right thumb into a spot where he knew he could shut off the artery. If he had time, he might fashion a tourniquet.

"Zavello."

He did not have time. He struggled to his feet and began running. It was not a stealthy run. He felt weak, lightheaded, sick to his stomach. Barely able to see ahead of himself, he did not waste even a half second trying to see what damage had been done to his arm, whether the hand still hung by threads, whether it might be found and attached.

He ran, as if in a dream.

And, as in a nightmare, he heard footsteps thrashing through the forest behind him, footsteps as unsteady as his own.

Maybe he had an edge still, if the Montagnard had taken the blast standing up.

He needed some kind of advantage. If the Montagnard caught up to him, he would have no trouble fighting a one-handed man. He might simply wait until Night Runner bled out, then finish him. He did not have to do a thing to win this battle except bring Night Runner to bay.

Night Runner forced his flighty mind to concentrate. What was his advantage? He had his night vision. He could still hear fairly well. Maybe if he got to the trail. He veered left.

He found the path in seconds and saw his escape as the tunnel of vision that he had imagined earlier. He tried sprinting but stumbled into a divot in the ground and fell, his mind willing to go faster than his knees could lift his feet. He snaked forward, down the trail a few feet farther. For a second, he thought he heard only silence behind him. Then a crash of that body through the foliage.

He turned and saw the Montagnard lying across the trail, groaning, having tripped on the same fresh hole in the ground. He saw the wounds, his right leg damaged, and strips of flesh peeled off his chest.

Night Runner wondered if he might roll over into the low bushes and remain silent. Maybe the Montagnard would bleed out first. Maybe he would not be able to find Night Runner, his superior senses having been blasted into oblivion by the concussion grenade. Maybe his enemy would give up.

The head turned. The eyes of the Montagnard locked with his own.

Maybe nothing. Night Runner needed a new option. The Montagnard got to his knees, his right hand clutching Runner's own weapon, the scimitar.

Still clutching his stump, Runner rolled to his knees and staggered to his feet, setting off down the trail again. Everything in his mind told him he was running just fine. But the sounds of his feet slapping on the trail told him otherwise. He was staggering like a drunk.

No radio, no weapons, no tools. The team would wait for him, perhaps send somebody back.

But how would they know where to find him?

Answer: they wouldn't. He had veered off the trail they had briefed.

He was in this alone.

He looked over his shoulder and saw the Montagnard coming, running with a limp, to be sure, but gaining ground on Night Runner just the same. Night Runner turned back toward the trail and ducked just in time to avoid an overhead branch that might have caught him by the throat, taking him down, leaving him helpless.

A surge of new life. Still, he realized he was not defenseless. He recognized where he was in the forest. As light as his head, as unsteady as his balance, as weak as his knees all were, he knew he might have a chance if he could get another fifty meters out of his legs. If only the vacuum at the core of his body, the emptiness he felt because of the loss of blood, could be overcome for a few more steps.

He concentrated on his heart, directing it to work in time with his mind, as if somehow that might stimulate his pulse and help circulate his blood.

He had a plan now. Just knowing that he was not running away from his enemy gave him a clarity of thought. He cut the distance he needed to go to forty meters. The faint hope that he might yet defeat the Montagnard gave him strength to halve the distance to twenty meters. A glimpse into his future, seeing the battle ahead with the bureaucracy so he could stay in Force Recon with a prosthetic hand, shoved him ten more meters. A look over his shoulder to see that the Montagnard had somehow found the energy to be run-

ning practically at his heels gave Night Runner one last burst
of power to finish his crippled, broken sprint.

TWO VOICES IN the forest growled their cries of victory. The
Montagnard because he had somehow kept his senses about
him enough to dive backward as he glimpsed the grenade in
the hand of the American those short minutes ago. His right
leg had caught in the foliage, yes. It had taken shrapnel. He
had lost blood. But he drew on his reserve of strength to
finish this fight, to chase down his quarry. And he had not
lost his reserve weapon, the switchblade dagger. Better yet,
he had the American's sword. What better way to kill a man
than with his own weapon?

He raised the weapon, poised to slash the back of his enemy, the finest individual fighter he had ever faced, but his
defeated enemy just the same.

He heard his man cry out. It sounded like a shout of tri-
umph instead of defeat, as if he had won the race, crossing
the finish line first. Why, the man even threw up his arms—
the Montagnard saw for the first time that he had only the
one hand—like a disabled sprinter waving to the crowd.

He saw the hand hit a vine, close on it, pull it like a
lanyard. He brought the sword down, aiming for the spot at
the juncture of neck and shoulder, not wanting a sudden kill.
Instead, hoping to disable the man's good right arm and kill
him at his leisure, make him suffer for what he did to the
tiger.

The curved blade passed through empty space. The American might have lost his left hand, but he still had a few
tricks left in him.

Somehow, he had seen the blow coming. Somehow, he
knew to dive.

The Montagnard saw a blur, something thrown at his head.
Something thrown too slowly to do any damage. He leaned
to his left, avoiding it easily.

Only when it passed by his head, did the Montagnard realize what the flying object was. At that instant, he knew he was dead, that he had lost the fight with the American, even before the concussion grenade, a booby trap not a foot from his ear, vaporized his head.

WHEN THE SECOND grenade went off, Friel was only twenty meters away in the forest, looking away from the blast. He dove toward the ground by instinct, but never made it. The tangle was so thick at that spot, the bushes caught him, bent, and sprang back, lifting him to his feet. Deafened, he turned his head to the left and right, watching for movement through his night vision goggles, which had not been washed out. Nothing.

He thought he could hear the helicopter behind him. Maybe it was just his imagination.

He pushed on toward the spot where the concussion grenade had gone off. He had heard boomers enough times. This was one of their own. The only thing he could not be sure of was, had Night Runner thrown it to defend himself, or had he walked into one of his own booby traps, one of the ones they set earlier that day?

He broke out onto the trail and practically fell on his face. One second he was pushing against the foliage. The next, it gave way. He dropped to one knee and swept the rifle right, then left. He could not stifle the cry of anguish that escaped his throat. There lay the headless Night Runner.

He could not stop himself from calling the name of the gunny, who had obviously killed himself with his own booby trap.

"Henry, we have to get out of here."

Friel nearly pulled down on the ghost that had materialized beside him on the trail.

"Chief?" He looked from the figure beside him to the corpse just twenty feet away, the figure pointing at the headless corpse.

"The Montagnard."

By now, Friel had seen the stump of his noncom's left
arm, strings of sinew and gore trailing from it and down
Night Runner's good arm, dripping off his right elbow. Friel
could not take his eyes off the jagged amputation. He
swooned, nearly keeling over, as his chin fell to his chest.

"Jeez, Runner."

"I'm all right, Henry." But Night Runner wasn't all right.
His legs crumpled, and he fell on his face.

Friel staggered to his feet, pulled off his belt, and fash-
ioned the loop of a tourniquet, using the handle of his bayonet to twist off the flow of blood. A strip of bad-ass duct
tape around the bloody forearm kept the blade from unwind-
ing.

As Friel pulled Night Runner to a sitting position so he
could lift him onto his shoulder, the gunny spoke. "You
saved my life, Henry."

"A dozen more times, and we'll be even, Gunny."

Night Runner whispered, "How did you know where to
find me?"

"Don't be messing with me, Gunny. I saw you standing
at the edge of the jungle waving for me to come on. I followed you. What else was I going to do?"

The only answer Night Runner could muster was a thank-
ful sigh.

EPILOGUE

CORPORAL NATHANIEL DAVID Greiner could not believe his eyes until he had taken a third, long look at Night Runner's stump. He felt his world crumble at the edges. The team had lost something here in Vietnam, a place where a disgrace as much as a war had been perpetrated. A place better known in his high school history book for the protests about it. The Spartans had lost their most effective soldier; surely they would not let the Gunny come back to fight in a condition worse than having one hand tied behind his back. Greiner felt ashamed. He was being selfish. All he had cared about was keeping the team together. What if he had Night Runner's problem? As the helicopter lifted off, he looked outside, presumably to provide security, to answer any fire that might come up from the ground. Really, he did not want to look at Night Runner. He doubted he would ever have to again.

SERGEANT HENRY FRIEL was both sick and sad. And proud of himself besides, if that wasn't too much of contradiction. Sick and sad that Night Runner had lost his hand, and maybe his position in the Marine Corps. But he was proud of his man, the warrior whom he knew could never be defeated, even at the cost of a hand. He was proud of himself, too. Because he had run from the LZ and into the jungle after Night Runner. Nobody chewed his ass once he insisted his gunny had waved to him. He saw no heroism in that. That was his job. Only one thing could he not figure out. Why didn't Night Runner just run to the helicopter? Why did he wave Friel back into the forest to get half his freaking hand blown off? As many times as he asked, Night Runner would not answer him about that. He acted more happy that Friel had saved his stupid freaking sword than his life.

CAPTAIN JACK SWAYNE let his emotions cycle like the whirlwind they were: fear, denial, hatred, anger, sorrow, disappointment, loss. If he had truly believed he might find his father—and he could not even tell whether he had felt it or fantasized it—he knew for certain that he had no father now. He hoped that the man had died a Marine, as he had always thought. He hoped that he had never been missing in action, captured, and kept in a POW camp for all these years. What a hell that must have been for those who went through it. For a while he had lost Zavello, too, who had become a kind of surrogate father, albeit of the verbally abusive variety. Then Night Runner, his brother. Good God, Night Runner. This team would not be the Spartans without him. Would the loss of a hand kill his spirit as well? Swayne decided Night Runner's future would determine his own. If the man left Force Recon, he, Jack Swayne, could not remain behind. He wasn't sure whether he could even remain in a Marine Corps that did not include . . .

GUNNERY SERGEANT ROBERT Night Runner, warrior of the Blackfeet nation and the United States Marine Corps. Friel had thrown him onto the deck of the cargo compartment of the Blackhawk as if he were a corpse. But Night Runner was conscious. When he rolled over onto his back, holding up his stump, Swayne looked as if he'd been kicked in the gut. The onboard medic found a vein and began running blood from a bag, already hung with Runner's name on it. Night Runner instantly felt at peace. He would get a prosthetic hand. And soon. He had turned to Zavello in the helicopter and told him—not a request, but a demand—"I'm staying in Force Recon." Then he closed his eyes, at peace because he had defeated the best warrior he had ever known, the Montagnard. Not necessarily because he had killed him. But because he would be a warrior on future Force Recon missions, whereas the Montagnard would never fight again. He gave a special thanks to Heavy Runner. First, for showing him a safe way down from the trees and into the camp. Second, for guiding Friel to him as he lay on the trail.

COLONEL KARL ZAVELLO had felt the imperative of going to Vietnam three times in his youth. It was something he had to get out of his system, something about finding out about his manhood, proving to himself and anybody else who needed to hear it that he was the complete Marine. This last time, his fourth, he knew was a mistake, even before he saw what it had cost Night Runner. He had come over on a lark, hoping to meet up with an old friend, wondering whether he could do one last good deed about Vietnam, a war he had not lost, a cause he had not dishonored. There had been prisoners left over. He thought he might save them after a lifetime of captivity. But he had proven himself no savior. Just as the Montagnard had proved himself no friend. For his foolishness, Zavello had gotten himself thrown into a prison camp, as if he were an unfinished item of business for the Vietnamese, rather than the other way around. He had reached out for the last resort of the Marine when his country, his unit, and his own training could not help him pull his ass out of the fire. He had reached out to God, that six-star Marine, praying that his capture would not cost the loss of the Force Recon unit. He had even dared to pray that, although he might look stupid after they got out of Vietnam, nobody would get hurt. He stopped praying in that the instant he saw Night Runner staggering through the grass, Friel's hand hooked under his good elbow, guiding him, holding him up, the stump waving like a broken flagstaff. Like him, Night Runner had been maimed. Like him, the gunny might never see combat action again, if he were even retained in the Corps. Night Runner, possibly the best fighting Marine he had ever met, now a one-handed man. He knew what Night Runner was feeling, had tasted the bitterness himself. He knew what he must do, the only thing possible to restore this situation. He would fight for this man, keeping him in the Marine Corps and assigned to Force Recon. If he couldn't get Night Runner back to the field, he would have to admit to having let down himself and this, the finest of Marine noncoms. He would have to quit in disgrace, live in disgrace, die in disgrace. He would personally shepherd Night Runner's comeback. Even if it would be his last mission as a part of Force Recon.

"Fasten your seat belt! *Carrier* is a stimulating, fast-paced novel brimming with action and high drama." —Joe Weber

CARRIER

Keith Douglass

U.S. MARINES. PILOTS. NAVY SEALS. THE ULTIMATE MILITARY POWER PLAY.

The Carrier Battle Group Fourteen—a force including a super-carrier, amphibious unit, guided missile cruiser, and destroyer—is brought to life with stunning authenticity and action in high-tech thrillers as explosive as today's headlines.

B384

DAVID ALEXANDER
MARINE FORCE ONE

*A special detachment of the Marine Corps whose prowess
in combat and specialized training sets
them apart from the average grunt. They charge where
others retreat, and succeed where others fail.
They are the best America's got...*

MARINE FORCE ONE
0-425-18152-9

As tensions continue to build between North and South Korea,
Marine Force One is sent on a recon mission that reveals North
Korea's plans to use chemical weapons against the south. But before
they can report to H.Q., they are ambushed and overwhelmed by a
relentless pursuit force.

MARINE FORCE ONE: STRIKE VECTOR
0-425-18307-6

In the deserts of Iraq, there's trouble under the blistering sun. Using
an overland black-market route that stretches from Germany to Iraq,
extremist forces have gathered materials to create a new weapon of
devastation. It's a hybrid nuclear warhead that needs no
missile—it can be fired from artillery. And it could cast a
radioactive cloud over the entire Middle East.

MARINE FORCE ONE: RECON BY FIRE
0-425-18504-4

To find the leaders of a terrorist organization, Marine Force One
heads to Yemen—but the terrorists have kidnapped an
American Air Force Officer—and getting close to
them puts his life in danger.

Available wherever books are sold or
to order call 1-800-788-6262